ISLAND FRUIT REMEDY

RICH SHAPERO

ISLAND FRUIT REMEDY

A NOVEL

HALF MOON BAY, CALIFORNIA

TooFar Media
500 Stone Pine Road, Box 3169
Half Moon Bay, CA 94019

Library of Congress Cataloging-in-Publication Data is available.

ISBN: 978-1-7335259-4-7

Cover artwork by Ramón Alejandro
Cover design by Adde Russell and Michael Baron Shaw

Additional graphics: Sky Shapero

Printed and Bound by CPI Group (UK) Ltd, Croydon, CR0 4YY

23 22 2 3 4 5

Also by Rich Shapero

Balcony of Fog

Rin, Tongue and Dorner

Arms from the Sea

The Hope We Seek

Too Far

Wild Animus

1

"We float together—unborn twins with shrinking tails and mucid limbs, clasping each other in an inky blur. Your shoulders glisten with garnet bubbles. Around your head, a halo of pearls; and as you nod, crepes of silk, onyx and gleaming, fold and furl. Roll in my arms, and I'll roll in yours, sheltered, fearless, gloating over our foodless feast; decked in treasure, enthroned together, our ivory serpents twisting between.

"The moment looms. We shudder, we shake. Nestling, squeezing, our artless bodies heave and convulse, and the rapture begins. A helpless frenzy, our violent trance, familiar, expected, but never the same. We curl, we roll—warm, viscous, swaddled in bliss, our oily cocoon, our midnight pool—mated and joined; one, not two."

In the darkened conference hall, the man's voice resounded, deep and doughty. A candle flickered, and above it his face was etched—precision lips, dewy eyes and an earnest brow.

"Those outside— What do they see?

"What do they know of this secret world, with waxen clouds, with silky fogs and moony glints, wrapped by stars with ductile arms, a Fabergé egg turned outside in. Our matchless home, this singular moment—

"What do they know of our fate, our faith, our Sacred Space?"

Slowly, the lights came up.

Applause started, and a sea of faces appeared, most of them female.

The man on the dais closed his book and pinched out the candle on the lectern. Then he stepped forward and bowed to the clapping crowd as they rose to their feet. His shoulders were broad, his legs long and thin. He tipped like a martini glass without a base as the admiration washed over him, thankful but shy. Some leaned toward him, as if to help him through his unease; others rocked on their heels, carried along in the dance.

He was in his mid twenties. His black hair mounted in a wave above his brow and swept back and around, like a fifties teen idol. His garb too—a sequined ricky jacket with an elastic waist, and cowboy boots—seemed borrowed from another time. As the applause subsided, his eyes turned childish, soft, venturing. A curl dropped over his forehead.

"Thanks," he said, scanning the faces in the hall, settling on one with a heartstruck cast. "I imagined those words sounding in darkness," he spoke directly to her, "and it was kind of you to let me offer them that way." A freckle-faced woman in the front row had her hands clasped beneath her chin. "It means so much to me," he focused on her, "that you see something in this 'idiosyncratic confession,' as my publisher calls it. He had some reservations."

Laughter, polite and sympathetic, crawled through the crowd.

"Have a wonderful three days here in Baltimore, and I wish you all prolific and rewarding meditations on your own Sacred Spaces."

As he removed his lapel mic, the emcee spoke from a corner of the stage, inviting attendees to cue up during the break. "Wood is available to sign *Unborn Twins*," she said, holding a copy of his novel upside down. Below the dais, books were piled on a table.

Wood hooked his arm over his head and snapped his wrist, like a kid in a cowboy fantasy twirling a rope. Then he descended the stage, sheltering his gaze.

A crowd gathered quickly behind the table. Wood touched his wedding band for luck and safekeeping, and the next moment he was surrounded by women asking questions, eyeing him with fondness and curiosity. Nodding, peeking, shaking hands, taking his seat, Wood felt their collected need. Some had ulterior motives, but most embraced Romance with genuine feeling. Each, like himself, had a hungry heart to nourish, and they sensed he had something of worth to share.

When the van pulled into the drive, Wood's car was there, but Vadette's was not. He thanked the driver and lugged his suitcase to the front door. The house had been built on the sand barrens, but the fog was thick and the dunes were hidden. He had tried Vadette from the hotel, and again from the airport before his flight. Wood imagined she'd be home when he returned. He turned his key in the lock and crossed the threshold.

"Vadette?"

No response.

"Are you here?" Wood pulled off his coat.

The house was chilly. Fog curtained the windows. He strode to the thermostat and turned up the heat. There was a note on the kitchen counter, with a saltshaker on it. When he removed the weight, the note curled in his hand.

"In Mazatlán with Barb," the note read. She'd signed it "V."

He was tired and hungry. When he opened the refrigerator, it was empty. He pulled a pound of burger meat out of the freezer and put it on the counter. It was odd she hadn't left a message on his phone.

He glanced at the note, then removed his phone from his pocket and called her. She didn't answer.

"Nice down there, I expect," he said. "San Diego's fogged in. Call me. I love you."

He made dinner for himself. After that he unpacked his things and transferred a few ideas for his second novel to his computer. As yet, the ideas were scattered, but his feelings for Vadette—missing her and the soleness they shared—helped bring a few of the pieces together. Slowly the new concept was taking shape.

It was a couple of hours before he returned to the counter. He picked up the note and scanned it, frowning. Then he set it down, grabbed his phone and called her again.

This time she answered.

"Hey," he said warmly.

"What is it?"

"You're in Mazatlán?"

"I needed a vacation," Vadette said.

"With Barb."

"Yes, with Barb. She rented a place for the week."

"Fiesta time," Wood said.

"Every day," Vadette replied matter-of-factly.

"Is something wrong?"

"No. Everyone's been very friendly."

"When are you coming back?"

"Saturday."

He felt like he was intruding.

"Well, have fun. Tell Barb hello for me. And Dave."

"It's over for them."

"What happened?"

"I'll tell you about it when I get back."

"Vadette—"

"Saturday, Wood."

"See you Saturday."

Wood put the phone down, wondering. She was there at Barb's request. Vadette needed a break, her job was demanding. He'd been absent a lot himself, promoting his book. However distant their bodies might be, their hearts were together.

He stepped into the living room and sat on the couch. Despite his effort to calm himself, doubts wormed through. For a few months now, Vadette had been distant. Before he left for Baltimore, they'd had a conversation that troubled him. She seemed disoriented. She said she'd been asking questions, questions she couldn't answer.

Could a rift have opened without his knowing? The idea seemed suddenly real. What was going on in Mazatlán? He watched the fog swirling beyond the picture window, concern mounting.

The next morning, Wood felt queasy, as if he'd spent the night at sea. He shaved and combed his hair, eyeing his worried face in the mirror. Saturday, she said. He put his pants on and opened his laptop. His readers were waiting.

He reviewed an assortment of scenes and moments he'd trialed, circling the larger question. Should he return to the theme of *Unborn Twins*? Did he have any choice?

After an hour, he stopped to eat, still bare-chested. He

returned to his computer, but it was hopeless. He couldn't concentrate.

He retrieved his phone and sat on the bed. He wasn't sure how to voice his concern. *If something's wrong,* he thought, *I should be cautious.*

He rang Vadette's number.

"Are things okay between us?" he asked straightaway.

"We'll talk about it when I get back."

"What's going on?"

"Not now," she said with irritation.

"I got this crazy idea last night—"

He stopped himself and waited for her to respond.

The silence stretched out.

"Can you come home?" Wood said. "I'm missing you."

"I'll be back on Saturday."

He heard her firmness, but his heart denied it.

"With a whisper the Space expands," he said softly. "Love blinds us and swallows the world."

"Please, Wood."

His lips parted. He shook his head. "Saturday then."

And the call ended.

Things were worse than he'd imagined.

The rest of the day, Wood was in a stupor. He stared at the fog, muddled over his notes and fell asleep on the couch.

When he awoke, the fog was thick against the living room window. A stray dog swam toward him, as if suspended in it.

He resisted the temptation to call Vadette, and the week dragged by. Finally Saturday arrived. At the airport, he was early and the plane was late. After a long wait, he caught sight of Vadette emerging from Passport Control.

It was an MGM entrance. She wore a scarlet dress with a wide-brimmed red hat and sunglasses, and was clearing an aisle for herself through the other passengers. Vadette was given to humor, and she was laughing, aware of the attention she was drawing. She recognized him with a wave, chin up, as if she was still in Mazatlán, greeting him from the foredeck of an arriving cruiser.

But as she drew closer her gaze shifted, and when he opened his arms to embrace her, she turned away.

In the car, he tried to start a conversation. Her finger toyed with a rose-gold curl by her neck. She gazed out the window, as if she couldn't hear a word he said. Beneath the chill in her attitude, Wood sensed a note of defiance.

As he pulled into the carport, he spoke harshly, insisting she say something. But a wall had been built, and she remained behind it.

He helped her with her bags. Vadette left the ones she was carrying at the hallway entrance. Wood did likewise and followed her into the bedroom. She removed the red hat and dropped it, top down, on the chair beside the dresser.

"Where did you find that?" he asked.

"It was a present."

She turned her back to him and removed her clothing. The sight of her naked body made him weak with longing.

"I'm exhausted," she said half to herself.

She moved past him and drew the drapes. It wasn't yet dark. Then she stepped to the far side of the bed and crawled beneath the sheets. "Can you get the light?" she said.

Wood regarded her for a long moment, then he threw the switch and darkened the room. The bathroom door was ajar, and the night lamp cast a golden blade through the gap. It crossed the carpet, touching the foot of the bed. He turned and strode into the living room.

Vadette rolled over, sighed and buried her face in the pillow. On the seat of the chair, the red hat trembled. Silently, very slightly, the broad brim shifted. Something that gleamed, the size and shape of a tweezer, emerged from the sweatband. It was a pincer—two opposable fingers. And then the rest of the creature appeared—a scorpion with a pair of small arms, a segmented body and a straightened tail. It scuttled over the hat brim, onto the chair seat and, from there, down the wooden leg to the floor.

The scorpion followed the blade of light across the carpet. It was three inches in length and red-brown, the color of coagulated blood. When it reached the hem of the comforter, it extended its pincers and clung. Its hind claws freed themselves, and the scorpion swung from the hem, tail curling. Then it was climbing the comforter, cresting the camber of the mattress, crossing the flat plain of the bedding. When it reached the counterpane, it skirted Vadette's elbow and disappeared beneath her pillow.

A moment later Wood returned. He regarded Vadette's motionless body, then removed his clothing and approached the bed.

"Vadette?" he said softly.

She didn't respond. Was she already asleep?

He drew back the covers and slid beside her. Not touching, but very close. He lay still for a moment, then he placed his hand on her hip.

No word or movement.

Was she conscious? If she wasn't—

Wood feared he would aggravate the situation, so he withdrew his hand and lay there, frozen, until sleep found him. Beneath the corner of Vadette's pillow, the scorpion crouched, facing Wood's head, ten inches away.

The next morning, he woke to the sound of the shower. He rose and opened the drapes. Fog. The valley below was lost in it. The sound of the shower ceased. After a minute of silence, he could hear Vadette drying her hair. Then the bathroom door opened and she stepped out with a towel around her. She smiled at him.

Wood drew a pair of briefs from the dresser and pulled them on.

She faced the mirror and brushed her hair, parting it in the middle. The gold strands were tinted carmine and fell in waves to her shoulders. Beneath the dark brows, her eyes showed nothing. Her small breasts trembled with the movement of her arm. He stepped close and circled her middle, feeling her softness. He kissed her cheek.

Vadette opened a drawer to retrieve her lingerie. Then she crossed to the closet and selected a dress. Wood watched in silence while she clothed herself.

Finally she turned. "I'll make some tea," she said, and she stepped through the doorway and down the hall.

Wood put on a pair of pants and found a fresh shirt. As he was buttoning it, the scorpion beneath Vadette's pillow crawled from hiding, scuttling across the comforter. Wood didn't notice. He retrieved a pair of socks from the dresser and sat on the edge of the bed to pull them on. The scorpion disappeared into a fold, then reappeared, headed toward his thigh. As Wood tied his shoes, the scorpion grabbed his pant leg, clinging to the seam, just below the pocket. Wood rose and walked into the dining area, carrying the creature with him.

In the kitchen, Vadette was by the stovetop, lowering a tea ball into the pot.

Wood stood watching for a moment, then sat at the dining room table. There were two napkins, each with a spoon on top. The scorpion climbed his waistband, onto his shirt, rising beneath his left sleeve and then onto it, making its way toward the elbow.

"Let me help you," Wood said. As he rose from his chair, the scorpion fell onto the table. It scuttled beneath one of the napkins.

Wood got two mugs from the cupboard, and a carton of half-and-half, and returned to the table with them. Vadette followed with the pot of brewed tea.

"I've been unhappy," she said.

Wood regarded her and nodded. He opened the carton of half-and-half and added some to each mug.

"Very unhappy," Vadette said, pouring the tea. She didn't sound unhappy. She was talking about her state of mind before leaving for Mazatlán. When the tea reached the brim of the second cup, she set the pot down. "We have to talk."

"Well, let's talk." Wood threw up his hands. "What's going on?"

She raised her brows and glanced aside, as if she'd been dreading this moment.

He stood. "You're treating me like a stranger."

She didn't flinch. She was braced for a reaction.

Wood grabbed her waist and pressed her to him.

"I'm not sleeping with you again," Vadette said.

Wood stared at her, and she at him. The scorpion scuttled from beneath the napkin. It crossed the tabletop, reached one of the mugs and climbed its side.

"I'm moving out," Vadette said.

"'We're finished.' Just like that?"

"Just like that," she said.

The scorpion reached the brim, teetered and plunked into the milky fluid, disappearing beneath the surface.

"Why?" Wood asked.

"You don't want to know."

"Try me."

She shook her head.

Wood eyed her with disbelief. He grabbed the mug with the scorpion in it and brought it to his lips, then set it back down, seething with gall. "I deserve better than this."

She circled the table to put herself out of reach. "I'm going to be late for work." She glanced at her watch.

"You're not leaving." He followed her.

She stopped in front of the mug with the scorpion in it. "Yes I am."

She slid her fingers through the mug's handle and raised it.

"Vadette—" Wood put his hand on her arm.

She shrugged free and drank, and she kept on drinking until there was nothing left. When she lowered it to the table, the mug was empty.

Then she turned on her heel and strode to the front door.

Wood tried to return to his notes. His idea, still vague, was to take the twins forward in time. Achievement would divide them—wealth, prominence, envy—but they'd find their way back to the Sacred Space. The passages he'd written seemed hollow and false, and the more he read, the worse he felt.

At noon the fog cleared, and he went for a walk on the dunes. Vadette called at the end of the day. She told him she was moving in with Festa, a friend in Solana Beach. She would be back the next evening to get her clothes. He asked if he could see her that night, if they could have dinner together. Vadette declined.

The following evening, she returned. While he watched, she transferred her clothing into suitcases and boxes she'd brought. She refused to talk until her car was loaded, but before she left, there was a brief thaw.

They stood in the doorway, and Wood again asked her why.

She took a breath. "I need more from life."

"I'm your twin. Whatever you need—"

"You see things the way you'd like them to be," she said, "not as they are."

"Vadette—"

"No," she shook her head, turning away.

He grabbed her arm. "We'll work it out."

"Work it out with another woman."

"I don't want another woman. I love you."

She laughed. "You don't care a thing about me. You don't know who I am."

"You're my other half, my reason for living."

Vadette closed her eyes. "I can't help it, Wood. Something snapped."

"Go ahead," he said bitterly. "Take your things. I never want to see you again."

Vadette's departure seemed impossible. They'd been blissful together for years, hadn't they?

He phoned her repeatedly during the days that followed. She refused to answer, and when he called Festa she fended him off. Wood was angry, disbelieving. He longed for Vadette's return, imagining things he would do to recapture her affections. There were a hundred questions he would ask her if she gave him the chance. At the end of the fourth day, he drove to Festa's and rang the bell.

Festa came to the door in her bathrobe, pasty and overweight. Before he could say a word, she stepped onto the porch. "She's not here," Festa said.

"Bullshit."

"You're not coming in."

"She's my wife."

"You have to respect her independence now. That's what she wants."

"We've hardly spoken," he said. "What's going on? What is she telling you?"

Festa took a deep breath. She looked like someone who'd

eaten too much at a long meal. “Being single isn’t easy,” she said. “You’ll survive.”

“Thanks for the advice,” Wood said acidly.

“You’ve taken everything from her,” Festa said, relenting. “She has nothing left. She wants to pick up a few more things from your house.” Festa eyed him with agitation. “Maybe tomorrow? Wood—” She folded her arms across her breasts, as if to protect herself. “It’s over. Try to accept that.”

Wood slept till noon the next day. When he rose, he stumbled to the back door and stepped outside, onto the sand barrens. Naked, he circled the house again and again. When he returned inside, he wandered the rooms, still naked, opening closets, pulling things off of shelves, picking through shoe boxes. Photos, gifts, objects they’d found, mementos of special moments and the life they’d built in the Space together— Using furniture he dragged into the living room, he arranged them chronologically. It was the Wood and Vadette Museum. The memories were sure to touch her.

But that night, it was Festa who came, not Vadette. She had a list, and she strode past the Museum without a word. Wood helped her find the items and carry them to her car. Vadette was out of town, she said. But Festa wouldn’t say why or where.

Three days passed, and then Vadette called. She had returned to Solana Beach.

Wood heard a note of tenderness in her voice. He begged to see her. She agreed. Vadette asked him to come to Festa's that evening. To smooth the way, Wood sent her a carefully worded text message pledging himself to the renewal of their marriage, whatever that might mean.

Then he got in his car and headed for the coast. He'd met Vadette in a restaurant near campus five years before. They were both students, struggling to get by.

He parked in front of the restaurant and walked in. It was still a noodle house, and the table was in the same spot. That fateful day, they had both come for lunch. While they were waiting for a table, Wood invited her to join him. He remembered the moment their eyes met. They seemed to recognize each other.

"I'm starving," he'd said.

"Me too," Vadette smiled.

The hunger went farther than lunch. They were both empty in so many ways, lonely and penniless. When the meal was over, she gave him her number.

From the noodle house, Wood drove to his old apartment, recalling the night they had first made love. The building was boxy and drab, but to his sentimental eye, it was a place of sanctity. It was afterward, in the bedroom, he had penned his first lines of love. The feelings outsized him, and the language seemed stilted. But he shared them, and Vadette was moved. From her wonder and tears, she gave it a name.

He arrived at Festa's at 8 p.m. When he knocked, Vadette appeared barefoot, wearing a chemise he had given her on her birthday three years before. She began to cry as soon as she saw him.

He moved to hug her, but she shook her head.

Did she want to go out? No, she didn't feel up to that. Was she going to invite him in? No, no, she shook her head, tears still falling. So she stood on the threshold with the door open, and he stood on the porch facing her. Wood didn't want to spook her. He tried to act calm, casual.

"Tell me," he said. "What did I do?"

"Nothing," she replied. "It's me. I've changed."

"I can change too."

"You're perfect the way you are," she said. "You made me very happy."

"You're not happy now. What's wrong?"

She turned away.

"All I need is the darkness and you." Wood spoke with the solemn devotion that had infused their love from the start.

Vadette reached her hand out.

He took it.

"I still love you," she said. She was silent for a long moment. "Can we sit in your car?"

"Sure."

They approached the vehicle, but before they reached it, she stopped.

"Here," she said, wiping her eyes. She stood on the gravel drive, facing him. "This is fine."

Something traumatic had happened or was about to happen. Wood could see that now. Her arms were shaking. Her hands were at her thighs, fingers crookt, nails digging in. She spoke with her face averted.

"I love you," she said. "I'll always love you. You know that, don't you?"

Fresh tears. She stood sobbing quietly to herself, looking so miserable that Wood closed the distance between them to comfort her. He embraced her, put his lips to her cheek. She didn't flinch. He coaxed her head onto his shoulder. It rested there for a moment, then she turned and buried her grief in his chest.

"I'm with someone else," she said.

Wood drew back.

The sun setting behind him painted her chemise scarlet. Its silk gleamed like chitin. As he watched, the creases shifted.

"Someone else?" he said.

Vadette quivered. Jointed legs sprang from her middle. Her arm rose, bristling with hairs, scissoring a pair of giant red fingers.

Wood blinked. He was imagining—

The scarlet legs twitched. The joints of her arm clicked as it extended. He shied just in time—the pincers lunged and scissored, trying to shear his head from his neck.

"He's helping me through this," the scorpion said.

Her sternites compressed and both arms spread. Vadette's neck shrank into her body, and the tubes in her mouth pushed out. Wood saw her segmented tail quiver and curl, arching over her head, a giant bent thorn at its end, the hollow tip beaded, dripping with venom.

"I'm sleeping with him," she said.

The thorn struck Wood full in the chest, driving inside him. He felt the toxin like an electric shock in every nerve of his body. Wrenching free, he staggered back, clutching his pectoral. The pain was terrible. The hellish creature shook its tail and flexed its claws as he stumbled toward his car.

Wood screeched around the curves of Camino Del Mar. By the time he reached the Dieguito bridge, his clothing was drenched. The shock of her words— He'd seen something monstrous. A disguise, a delusion—

The face he saw in the rearview mirror was lathered with sweat, and the eyes were black with dread. On either side of the road behind him, giant scorpions rose, barring his return. The sting was deep. Around the wound, his chest was clenching. He gripped the wheel and forced the accelerator to the floor.

As he pulled into his carport, the spasms spread to his arms and legs. It was a struggle to open the front door. Once inside, he headed for the kitchen, turned on the tap and held his face under it. He was feverish, thirsty. He drank and drank. When he righted himself, he couldn't find his breath.

Wood reeled into the living room and tore off his shirt. The puncture was bleeding, the flesh around it hot and swollen. He grabbed his phone and collapsed on the sofa, searching his contacts, the toxins twisting his windpipe, tying his guts in knots. "Herb—" An acquaintance, an endocrinologist at Scripps who'd weathered a devastating infidelity. Someone picked up.

"Herb, it's Wood."

"I was just thinking of you."

Wood did his best to explain. Strangely, Herb took his story in stride.

"Let's check your pulse," Herb said.

Wood found it with his fingers and counted.

"Not good," Herb told him. "How's the stomach?"

"Awful. I'm going to throw up."

"You sound like you're having trouble breathing."

"I am."

"Unzip your pants and take a look at your dick."

Wood did as he said. "My god," he gasped. "It's huge."

"Alright," Herb said, "here's what we're going to do."

After some deep breathing to reduce Wood's heart rate, Herb sent him back to the kitchen to wash the wound and apply ice packs to his chest. That would stem the swelling, Herb said, and slow the spread of the venom. Then he had Wood lie on the sofa with his head elevated. By then, Wood was shivering and hearing voices.

"The neurotoxins," Herb told him, "are fucking with your head."

Herb shared his own experience. An unexpected attack, more like a serpent's bite, but the symptoms were similar. "You'll recover from the wound," he said. The pain would pass, and the puncture would heal. But the venom might have long-term effects.

"You're going to have to know more about the creature that stung you," Herb said. "And why. There's no way around that."

It took three days for the effects of the sting to abate. As mad as Vadette's transformation seemed, Wood had no choice but to accept it. Herb visited in the evenings. His objectivity, his pipe and knit cardigan, and the wry humor that shook his silver hair, made the injury manageable. Herb still lived with the creature that bit him. Somehow he'd made his peace with her.

"You feel like the offended party right now," Herb said, "but you probably bear some responsibility for what's happened. Whether or not you can put the marriage back together, there are questions you need Vadette to answer."

"I tried," Wood said.

"You need to try harder." Herb handed him the phone.

Wood called, but Vadette wouldn't answer. After a half-dozen attempts, Festa returned the call.

"It's over," she said, "O-V-E-R."

Herb motioned, and Wood passed the phone to him.

"I'm a friend of Wood's," Herb told her. "This is difficult

for him, as you might imagine. It would be a great help if you could answer a few questions. Can I put you on the speaker?"

Festa assented.

"Wood and Vadette have a lot of history together," Herb said. "This relationship she's formed— How new is it?"

"She met the man in Mazatlán. He's an American. He lives in L.A."

"They just met," Herb said.

"She's leaving on Friday. She's moving in with him. She asked me to tell Wood that she's happy with the clothing and personal items I picked up the other day. She doesn't need or want anything else. Wood is free to do what he likes with the furniture and their other possessions."

Herb raised his brows.

"She contacted an attorney yesterday. He's drawing up divorce papers," Festa said. "She wishes Wood well, but she doesn't want to speak to him again. Is that clear enough?"

"We appreciate your candor. These things are hard."

When the call ended, Herb looked at Wood. "It doesn't look good."

"I can't imagine life without her," Wood said.

"If she won't talk to you—" Herb dangled his hands between his knees, his face pinched. "That will make things harder."

As Herb predicted, the swelling in Wood's chest and groin subsided and the wound began to scab over. But he couldn't put Vadette or the sting out of his mind. The house seemed haunted now. There was pain in the walls, and the Museum was a cavalcade of atrocities. He imagined himself in a different town, a different state. But when he spoke to Herb, the older man cautioned him not to leave.

"You're too weak," Herb said. "The venom is still inside you."

"I have to get out of here," Wood replied.

He called the landlord, explained the situation and begged his way out of the lease, promising he would leave the furniture and kitchen items behind for the next tenant.

Then he found the atlas, opened it on the kitchen table and began to scroll through his phone contacts, looking for a destination. The phone slipped from his hand and struck his big toe. When Wood picked the phone up, a number was ringing.

"Who is this?" a groggy voice answered. "Wood?"

Wood looked at the phone to see who he'd dialed. "Cameron." It had been years since they'd spoken. "I'm calling from San Diego."

"Too long," Cameron said.

"Exactly," Wood answered. He massaged his toe. It was pink. "How's life," he opened the contact, "in Key West."

"Crazy as ever," Cameron said. "How about you?"

"I've been better," Wood said. "You remember Vadette?"

"Sure."

"Our marriage went bust. I'm through here. I've always wondered what Key West was like."

"Your timing's perfect," Cameron said. "I'm leaving for Cambodia tomorrow night. You can stay at my place if you like."

Florida. It would put the whole continent between him and Vadette. The tropics, gators and pirates, sand and foam—The idea seemed farfetched, like a boyhood fantasy. "You're serious."

"Why not?" Cameron said. "You'll be inspired here. The Key's a magical place."

2

Wood drove for twenty-seven hours without eating or sleeping. The car's trunk was stuffed, and his clothes were piled on the seats. With the windows up and the air conditioning on, he crossed the state lines in a soap bubble, feeling truly alone.

Outside of Biloxi, he stopped at a roadside diner. He wasn't hungry, but he ordered a cold drink to go. The sun was blistering hot and he was sweating, and when he tossed down the icy liquid, his heart rang like a gong. He staggered to a shady area beside the parking lot and collapsed in the grass.

He reached Tallahassee in the middle of the night and pulled into a campground. Grabbing a coat for ground cover, he tumbled out of the car and slept beneath a tree. Before noon the next day he hit Jacksonville, passed through Miami without stopping, and followed the signage to the Overseas Highway.

He found himself zooming up a ramp into a turquoise sky, then down, down to a place where boats were berthed, a flat raft of land circumscribed by the sea. On the island's far side, another bridge extended. This one skimmed water that was milky green. For the first time since leaving San Diego, Wood lowered his window, feeling a balmy breeze and cool spray. He leaned his head out and squinted, imagining he'd passed from a world that was lethal and dying into one that was fresh and benign.

For three hours, islets appeared one after the other, bridges mounting and dipping like a fun park ride. Finally, as if to herald his arrival, a rosy sun set behind clouds scrolled like pink taffy. But the felicity ended abruptly. His chest began to spasm again. The pain reached his hands and feet, making them twitch. Herb's parting advice had been, "You need to mend," and Wood muttered, "I'll mend here," sending his words into the wind like a prayer.

He crossed the last bridge, landed on Key West and followed the road into Old Town. Amid a maze of narrow streets, he found the small shuttered house and pulled into the drive. His head was throbbing, his stomach in knots. The door key was under the mat.

After a look inside, he lugged a suitcase and an armful of clothing to the bedroom. As he entered, a wave of dizziness broke over him, and the clothes and suitcase fell to the floor. Wood collapsed on the bed and lay there gasping. He regained his feet and stumbled to the bathroom to inspect his wound in the mirror. The scab hadn't cracked, the sting seemed to be healing. He had to get his mind off the pain.

He returned to the bedroom, picking some clothes from the pile, a pair of stovepipe jeans and a western vest with a two-tone yoke and smile pockets. He struggled them on and left the house. On the sidewalk, he could feel the venom in his veins, hot and glowing like copper wire; but the simple act of putting one foot ahead of the other calmed him. It seemed a triumph his body still worked.

No one would have guessed his condition. His back was straight. He stood tall and looked sure as ever. His prominent cheekbones, straight brows and cloven chin were signs of vigor, as were his brown and muscular arms. In the glancing light, his hair bulged and swirled like the heights of a trunk, as if the burnished locks were about to send boughs in every direction.

The streets were lined with homes from the Victorian era. Their shaded porches, ornate turrets, widow's walks and gingerbread facades were signs of a life removed, fanciful, lenient. As Wood approached the main drag, the crowds grew. Beach bums, tourists in bright clothing, young and collegiate, older and natty, ragged and homeless—

At the corner, he stopped and raised his head, seeing streetlights. When he lowered his gaze, he was peering at a pile of bright confections. Windows, shops. He continued down the block. A tipsy couple passed, a man with a shaved head and a woman with a giant pink ribbon in her hair. The woman grabbed his arm. "Refugio," she winked and pointed.

Wood ignored her. Then the wind blew him into the

street. Cars honked. On the far side, a pink cab was parked by the curb. The driver stood beside it, wearing a skipper's hat, and he tipped the visor as Wood approached. The neon behind him said *Refugio*. The windows were slatted with blinds.

Wood opened the door and stepped inside.

The place was dark and small, but packed. There was music, strumming and shakers, and a latin voice crooning over the babble. The patrons were hunched together, at each other's ears, shouting to be heard. Heads turned to follow him, drawn by the black bouffant, his martini frame and the bare arms and vest.

Wood's throat was tight, his legs brittle as matchsticks. Feeling awkward and watched, he slid onto a vacant stool by the bar. He hadn't been alone in a place like this since his college days. At the mercy of strangers now, he was as far from the Sacred Space as a soul could get.

A bartender turned, small, sleek and busty with blond hair. With a flourish, she raised a goblet and poured pink slush from a blender. She was wearing a bikini top that hid very little.

"It's okay, honey." She glanced at him. "You can look."

"Sorry," he muttered. "I just got here. My woman left me."

"Mine too," the bartender said. "She was a cheater."

Her lips were like mustachios, curving up from the midline, dipping deeply and rising again at the tail. She looked wistful, whimsical, as if she'd lived through her sorrow and come out the far side.

"She was looking for Papaya," the bartender said.

"Who's Papaya?"

"Are you thirsty?" she asked.

"What's that?" He nodded at the drink in her hand.

"An island blush," she said. "Rum, coconut cream and grenadine."

"I'll have one. I'm Wood."

"I'm Mango. Welcome to the Key."

He watched while she poured rum and grenadine into the blender. Her arms were finely sculpted, sleek and gently shouldered, and her movements were self-assured. If Mango had been wounded in love, she'd recovered; or found a way to mask the damage.

The blender's rumble ceased. She poured the slush into a goblet and set it before him. "A few of these," she said, "and you'll be back on your feet."

Wood laughed. As Mango stepped away, he lifted the drink. The glass was cool and round, filling his hand. The crushed ice prickled his tongue, and the coconut cream went down smoothly. It coated his throat and soothed the pain in his chest. When the rum hit his stomach, it warmed his core. *I'll be alright*, he thought.

"Hey there." A wet voice purred in his ear.

Wood turned without lowering the goblet. Through the foamy residue he saw an older woman in a faded dress. The bodice was loose and off-center, exposing her wrinkled cleavage. As he lowered his glass, she circled his back with her arm.

"You're safe with me," she said.

"Good to know," Wood replied.

Her hair was pixied and thatched, like a nut-brown swimming cap. She put a gift-wrapped box on the bar, then she pressed against him and kissed his cheek. "One of my boys," she announced to those nearby.

A man snorted. Another with a beard rolled his eyes. A third in paint-splattered overalls leaned close. "Don't mind her," he said.

The old woman had both hands on him now. "I'm your Auntie."

What luck, Wood thought. "I like having a relation in town."

"I'm not kidding. Buy me a drink."

Her features were thick—her nose and lips, her arms and breasts too. Everything about her seemed overinflated.

"Alright," he nodded. "What'll it be?"

"One of those." She eyed his goblet.

Wood waved at Mango. "A blush for Auntie." He felt the old woman's breast against his elbow.

"Take care of me," Auntie said. "I'll take care of you."

Mango glared at her, raising her arm, pointing at the door.

Auntie pouted. "No blush?"

Mango shook her head.

The old woman squeezed Wood's shoulder. "I'll be around. Don't you worry." Then she turned to go.

"Don't forget this." Wood handed the gift-wrapped box to her.

She pinched his cheek and took it. Then she edged through the crowd, headed for the door.

When Wood reached for his drink, he noticed a card on the bar. On it was written, "To my favorite, with fondness and gratitude." A man's name was signed.

He guzzled the blush. Above, the ceiling was an electrified forest, tear-shaped bulbs glowing emerald and lime at the ends of varnished branches. Lower down, the walls were painted with boulders, and beyond them was a breaking surf. Three blushes later, the bulbs were pulsing, and he could hear the surf through the music. He was about to order another when he noticed a woman standing beside him.

She was short with a swarthy complexion and blood-red lips. Green hair sprouted from a topknot on her crown. She had a stud in her lower lip and a line of them over one brow. She faced him, her eyes all pupil.

"Going to a square dance?" She touched his vest.

Wood didn't reply.

The woman's fingers crawled onto his bicep.

"I'm tanked," she said, wrinkling her nose. She stood on her toes to inspect him. "Are you a good guy?"

He saw fear in her eyes, like a bird on a branch, about to fly.

"I don't want to walk to my car alone," she said. "Go with me."

As he straightened, the fearful eyes glanced at the door. She seemed in earnest. "Okay," he said, pulling a few bills from his pocket and setting them on the bar.

The woman turned, and Wood followed her through the crowd.

On the sidewalk, she faced him. "I have some for you." She patted her purse. Her left shoulder was tattooed with a jungle scene. Snakes and lianas wound down her arm.

"Some what?"

"Meth." She swayed as if a storm was raging around them.

Wood grasped her arm. "You sure you can drive? Which is yours?"

She scanned the street and pointed.

"Thanks," she said when they reached her car. The door was bashed and the fender was hanging. She looked up and down the street while she fished for her keys.

"What are you afraid of?" he asked.

"Get in. I'll drive you back."

Wood did as she said. She started the engine and wove down the street, past Refugio.

"That's my stop," Wood said.

"I'm gonna take you home with me."

Wood stared at the woman, surprised, feeling the gulf between her and Vadette. An urchin, a meth head, sex hatched in a bar— Without warning, the pain came again, sharp and piercing. He looked down, expecting to see blood leaking through his vest.

"What's your name?" he muttered.

"Piña," she said.

"Let me out at the corner."

"You sure?" She put her hand on his leg.

It had gold nails, and there were rings on every finger. Wood could feel its warmth through the cloth. "I'm sure."

Piña pulled over.

"Thanks." He opened the door and stepped out.

As the car sped away, he started back down the street. A minute later, he turned on himself. He was a fool to rate Piña against his wife. Vadette was gone. He was starting life over. He should have let Piña take him home with her.

The idea choked him. *Vadette—* A sob rose in his throat.

Vadette, Vadette— He longed for her and the Sacred Space. Why did she do it? She'd ruined their lives. They would never find a love like that with anyone else.

Something grabbed his vest from behind. Wood turned, seeing a grizzled face, greasy hair, broken teeth and a juddering jaw. No words, just eyes that glared and a liquored breath. He grabbed the drunk's wrists and tore him loose.

"Papaya," the man leered.

Wood continued forward. The man kept pace beside him, dragging his leg.

"Where is she?" the drunk demanded.

Wood pretended he wasn't there.

"Hey," the man snarled. His bloodshot eyes were wide with suspicion.

"I don't know her," Wood said.

"You're lying," the drunk growled. Then he spied two sailors on the sidewalk ahead. He grunted and staggered toward them, waving his arm. "Papaya," he bellowed.

Wood slowed and ducked beneath a shop awning, uneager to be accosted again. As he watched, the drunk disappeared down the street, his rankled cry fading. “Papaya, Papaya, Papaya.”

The next morning, he unloaded the rest of his clothing and baggage. He’d missed meals for days, but he put food out of his mind and removed his computer and folders of notes from a suitcase, arranging them on the kitchen table. He plugged in the computer and sat down.

The pain from his wound had diminished, but when he entered the world of the twins and their Space, his mind froze. The words seemed foreign, written by someone else. After staring at the screen for an hour, he showered and shaved. Then he put on some shorts and a two-tone bowling shirt and left.

He found himself on Duval, drifting past shops, watching the passersby. He struck up a conversation with a lady at a cigar stand who suggested Las Nubes. The restaurant had a brunch party on an outdoor patio, with live latin music and a view of the water. He thanked her and bought a cigar. Two blocks down the street, the music reached him.

As he entered Las Nubes, Wood saw a man in a pink dress turning sheets of white paper into boat-shaped hats, crowns peaked like sails. Everyone was wearing them. The bobbing heads, with the sea behind them, looked like a toy regatta.

Wood donned his boat hat, strode to the bar and ordered a blush. On the counter beside him, someone had built a tower with playing cards. Drink in hand, he moved through the crowd. Two women stood on the patio together—attractive women, both in bright cottons, dark-eyed and curvaceous.

He was apprehensive, but he remembered Piña. I need to stop acting like a married man, he thought. He was on his own now.

Wood stepped toward the women and stopped before them. He greeted one.

She acted like he wasn't there.

He took a breath, smiled and raised his voice.

At that, the woman launched into a diatribe in Spanish that turned heads. Wood didn't understand a word she was saying. He was speechless, regretful, queasy.

A couple nearby eyed the dress-down with amusement. They had drinks in their hands. When Wood flushed and bowed, they toasted him. He stumbled toward them.

"Beaten, but valiant," the man laughed.

"Fearless," the woman nodded.

"I'm new at this," Wood said.

"No," the woman flared her eyes with mock surprise. She was jet-haired, nervy.

"I'm Tray." Square-jawed and big-chested, the man's lips were straight, but his face was still laughing. His eyes did the job.

"Mamoncillo," she extended her hand. "'Bijou' to you."

Their words were interrupted by the popping of firecrackers. Tray cocked his boat hat. On the boardwalk below, bicyclers raced by. Bijou pulled a large crucifix on a chain from beneath her shirt and used it to stir her drink.

"Where's your wife?" Tray asked.

Wood frowned. Was it that obvious? "San Diego," he said. "Or L.A."

"Separated?"

Wood nodded.

"'Anillo de boda,'" Tray smiled. "That's what your señorita was shouting. 'Wedding ring.'"

Wood looked at the gold band around his third finger.

"Till death do us part," Bijou said.

"That was the idea." Wood slid the ring off.

"A commitment," Bijou said, "some men can't make."

Tray groaned. Bijou pinched his side.

Wood slipped the ring into his pant pocket.

They traded some history. Bijou was a registered nurse. She worked at an urgent care clinic. Tray, a bit older than Wood, was a psychologist who did therapy on the Key.

"He's brilliant," she told Wood.

Tray nodded, agreeing.

"It's true," Bijou said. "Without Tray, the Key would be—"

"Alright," he laughed, "that's enough."

It was Wood's turn, so he talked about his writing.

"Romance pays the rent," Tray guessed. "You're working on something serious?"

"Nothing's more serious than love."

"Who reads your books?" Tray asked, deadpan.

"Overweight, frustrated, middle-aged women," Wood answered.

Their eyes met, and the two men laughed.

"Don't be mean," Bijou said.

"That's what he was thinking," Wood defended himself. "My readers have one thing in common." He turned back to Tray. "Their hearts are hungry. Some read to avoid the real thing; for them, words are enough. Others are braver, finding their way with a partner, testing their experience against my own. The bravest seek something unique. They're the ones I care about most."

"Unique?" Tray cocked his head.

Wood nodded. "People who seek a love no one before them has ever known."

Tray was sober now. It was Bijou who was laughing.

"What's so funny?" Tray said.

"You are," she replied, and she kissed his cheek.

They cruised the buffet together, talking about life on the Key.

"I'm curious," Wood said. "Why is everything pink?"

Bijou touched her middle. "Pink is the color of new life."

After they'd eaten, they exchanged phone numbers. As they parted, Tray grasped Wood's shoulder. "You're going to find what you're looking for."

Bijou turned. "I'm having some friends over on Wednesday. Why don't you come?" She glanced at Tray. "Maybe Tamarind." Bijou smiled at Wood. "She's smart, and she's a reader."

An hour before the start time for Bijou's party, Tray called Wood and offered to pick him up. As Wood seated himself, Tray handed him a joint, and they smoked while Tray jetted his sports car with the music at peak. Without a boat hat on, the therapist looked different. The bottom of his face was square, but the top was rounded and blond, an airy crown for the laughing eyes.

"Twenty-two?" he wondered. "You *are* an idealist."

"We had a rare affinity," Wood said.

"I've been with Bijou for six years."

"I knew the moment we met," Wood said. The irony echoed in his ears.

"'Love is a striking example of how little reality means to us.' You like Proust?"

Wood shook his head. "Too feeble, too passive."

"Sometimes we act. Sometimes the world acts on us. By the way—" Tray turned a corner and slowed. "Tamarind read your book."

"Good." Wood frowned.

Bijou's house was an old clapboard two-story. When they entered, a dozen friends were gathered around the dining room table, watching a short-haired woman hunched over, reading tarot. Bijou left the gathering and another onlooker joined her. The two women stepped toward them together.

Tamarind was small and slight, but buoyant and keen.

Her hair was dark, and her eyes sticky. She wore a wrap of buff linen, and her breasts were like beans beneath it.

She introduced herself and shook Wood's hand.

"From the west, I see." Tamarind eyed his boots and the buckskin stars woven into his powder blue coat. "The old west." She smiled.

"I came here in a time machine."

Bijou ushered Tray away.

"I love eccentricity." Her eyes softened. "And integrity. Bijou knows. It's a pleasure to meet you. I spent last night and the night before with you and your twin."

Wood saw the problem before him now.

"Should I ask what you think?"

"It was riveting. You created your own paradise." There was a note of envy in Tamarind's voice.

"Last month, those words would have meant a lot to me."

"And now?"

"The reality didn't live up to the fiction."

"Their innocence was endearing." Tamarind raised her hand and guided her hair behind her ear. "Most of us lose that quickly."

"You're in Old Town?"

She nodded. "I'm a yoga instructor. I came here tonight from the Bear Den."

Wood shook his head.

"A nude resort for gay men." She smiled and touched his bolo tie. "You're a character."

Wood drew back.

“I’m sorry.” She buckled her lips. “I’m curious. I can’t help myself.”

He was glad for the attention, but her adhesion rattled him. He escorted her to the tarot reading and broke free. But she kept her eye on him. Whenever he glanced in her direction, she met his gaze. And from time to time, she drew closer. He would be mid-sentence and find her standing beside him, listening as he spoke or laughing when he said something to amuse others.

Bijou had an activity planned. They were going to Mallory Square to see a friend of hers do magic tricks, and then they would walk the harbor. Wood went with Tray. The Square was crowded, and a dozen performers vied for attention. One juggled on a high wire, another did acrobatics with trained housecats. There were musicians, a sword swallower, Bible Bill, and the magic show.

As the sun set, Bijou led them along the coast. Boats were coming in, threading the blinking reef buoys. A group of night divers loaded their tanks onto a darkened schooner. The moonless sky, the fading chime of steel drums, the lapping of the tide—

Wood had lagged. Tamarind was walking beside him. Her presumption had vanished. There was a comfortable space between them, and her calm matched the night’s. As they passed a dock light, her features surprised him. The delicate line of her nose, the silky cheek, the shallow between eye and temple. She was a beautiful woman.

The walkway skirted a boat ramp, made private by a

cable. Bijou and the others were ahead, out of sight. Wood stopped by the cable, straddled it and took Tamarind's hand to help her over. They ambled along the dock admiring the yachts, and when they reached a locker, Wood invited her to sit beside him.

"How much did Bijou tell you?" he asked.

"You're separated. Your wife is with another man. The future's uncertain."

"It was sudden," he said. "And painful." Obliquely, metaphorically, he spoke of the baleful thing that had risen against him, of the sting and the venom, and fears that the poison was still inside him.

"*Unborn Twins*— I still believe two people can be that close." Beyond the moored yachts, the moonlit swells rippled.

"It's what we dream of," Tamarind said. "We come into the world crying and hungry. All of us." She drew a breath and shared a crushing disappointment of her own, a passion unreturned, a future unfulfilled. As she spoke, Wood fell in love with her voice. She was hurt, but brave; earnest and wistful. "Sometimes I think I'll never get over him," she said.

Wood turned to her, feeling like a child. Her eyes were soft and full of doubt.

"I need someone like you," he said.

"Do you?"

He nodded. "I really do."

The night's silence filled the space between them. They listened together for what seemed a long while. The torches of fire dancers twirled in the sky above Mallory Square.

He rose and reached for her hand. Tamarind stood without speaking. His lips lifted at the tails, then halted. He tried again, risking a smile.

"Do you want to spend the night with me?" she asked.

They pulled up to her apartment and the engine noise died. Neither spoke. Wood opened the car door without looking at her.

Inside, she led him to a sofa, saying she was going to change and use the bathroom. "Would you like to undress?" she said as she turned.

Wood watched her disappear down the hallway. Then he took a breath, unbuttoned his pants and looked down. It had been through a lot. Would it still work? He buttoned back up and began to pace the room.

Tamarind returned a few minutes later, wearing a sheer peignoir. She could see how troubled he was. She took his hand and steered him back to the sofa. They sat down together, and she removed his shoes.

"You're nervous," she said.

He nodded.

He'd had little experience with women before his wife. They'd been one, not two; and now he was half a person. Even those treasured intimacies were suspect. Tamarind was a stranger. Her thoughts, her emotions, her sounds, her scents—

She touched his chest. The sting twinged, and his fear spiked. The changed Vadette, that monstrous specter, was rising before him, mantling his mind. He could see her pincers, her arcing tail. He could feel the thorn's stab and the venom coursing inside him. His pulse faltered, his legs quivered. He planted them and stood.

Tamarind stood with him, confused. Was he leaving?

Wood didn't know. Maybe he was. "I'm sorry," he mumbled.

He was dizzy, his brow was damp. He reached for her shoulder. Tamarind braced him, putting her lips to his ear. "You're safe with me," she whispered.

"Am I?" His eyes searched hers.

She found the front of his pants and undid his buttons.

Wood felt her breath on his neck.

"You look ready to me," she said.

Wood tried to laugh. She put her arm around him and led him down the hall, into her bedroom.

He watched while she lit a pair of candles on the dresser. Then she turned, removed her peignoir and stepped closer. She undressed him slowly, without a word. When he was naked, she pressed her body to his.

"I'm lucky," he said, "that I'm with you."

"I'm nervous too."

"Are you?"

She nodded. "The Sacred Space."

He didn't reply.

"I'm worried I won't measure up." She looked into his eyes.

"The problem—" Wood stopped himself.

"Is there a problem?"

"It's all I know." He felt like a fool.

Tamarind kissed him. "We'll be teenagers. We'll pretend it's the first time."

She turned off the lights, stepped toward the bed and pulled back the sheets. Then she crawled onto the mattress and raised her arms to receive him.

Wood approached slowly, put a knee on the bed and lowered himself, reaching for her waist. He felt her hands settle on his back.

"There now," she whispered.

Her body seemed to soften beneath him.

"Have you ever slept with a Tamarind?" she said.

"You're the first."

"I didn't accept it when I was younger."

Wood felt her guiding him in.

"But as I ripened," she said, "I understood."

Wood kissed her neck.

She put her lips to his ear. "Go on. It's alright."

He eased himself deeper.

"Look," she said.

Wood could feel her fingers at the base of his spine.

"Look around you," she said.

Was she asking for something? What did she mean?

"Can you see the leaves?" she said.

An inner eye peered, and a night opened up—a night with shifting shadows.

"Can you see the leaves?"

The dark air was hung with sprays, twigs with leaves in double rows, tiny and green, like feathers on an arrow.

"Can you hear?" she whispered.

The feathered sprays hissed in the wind.

"Breathe through your nose," Tamarind said.

Wood did as she said, and he smelled damp soil.

"Wood and Tamarind," she whispered. "I'm with you now." Her voice was achingly tender. "Do you see? You're looking right at me."

Sprays like scarves, latticed and layered, webs of green—Hanging among them was a tassel of pods.

"I'm shy," she said.

The hidden Tamarind hung from a branch in an unseen world. Reticent, tentative.

Wood was baffled. Was the magic in her or the Key? Or had the sting of Vadette so scrambled his senses that he would never see women clearly again? He closed his eyes, parted his lips and drew a slow breath.

"Don't be afraid," she said. "Try me."

The tassel was still before him, a clutch of fawn-brown pods amid sighing sprays.

"Please," she said.

He stared, pulse pounding, ardor rising. He reached for a pod.

"Gently," she whispered.

The pod came loose in his hand. He held it, feeling its velvety surface. He pressed his thumb against it, and the brittle case broke, fragments clicking. Inside was the fruit, dark and gluey.

"Go ahead," she said.

He brought it to his lips and licked. The tart pulp met his tongue.

Wood drew back, stunned, and the spell broke. The candles flickered. Her sigh filled the room.

What did it mean? Why was she offering herself? To allay his hunger, for his pleasure in eating?

It was fear he felt, fear and guilt. The guilt of a man breaking faith with his wife. The fear of a man with poison inside him. Fear of disease, fear of not pleasing or not being pleased. Fear of hunger, its danger and the damage it did—

"Wood," she whispered, calling him back.

A fresh tassel of pods was hanging before him. Leaves were stuck to them. He peeled them away. His years with Vadette—silences, mysteries, deeds and pacts— That belonged to the past. He pulled a velvet pod loose and cracked it open.

His fingers touched the maroon mass. He pinched it, feeling it yield. Dense, sticky— Wood held the fruit to his nose, drawing its scent. Subtle, a mingling of odors he couldn't unbind. Again he touched his tongue to it, and again the tartness. Foreign, piquant, sour and sweet. He savored the taste and licked again. And again and again.

Wood put the sticky mass in his mouth and closed his jaws around it. The sharp flavor drew saliva from beneath his tongue. Tamarind was drowning in it. Her gummy mass was dissolving to syrup. And the creature of flesh? Were her breasts flattening? Thighs dwindling, hips narrowing, waist shrinking— Tamarind was melting in his mouth.

Wood stifled his relish, trying to preserve her, lifting her up, pushing her against his palate, shifting his tongue to keep his drool away. She gave and gave, sharper and sweeter as she shrank.

A new flavor was waiting at her center, new and unexpected. It stirred him. An inmost taste from the small bit of pulp that remained. Here it was now, terribly tart, unbearably sharp. Wood grew covetous, greedy—

Then the moment arrived. The last flitch slid between his molars, and he clamped and ground it, filling his mouth and mind with Tamarind's essence, consuming her completely. It was as if all that tang, those maddening tastes and gluey textures, had been created expressly for him.

Groaning, heart thumping, Wood closed his eyes, drawing long breaths.

"Did I hurt you?" he muttered.

"Hurt me?"

Her voice reached him, puzzled, astonished.

He turned, hearing the dying hiss, seeing the sprays feather and fade. In the darkness, on the damp earth, two bodies lay.

Still whole and alive, a creature of flesh— Tamarind was curling against him, soft and pliant, as if his greed had pleased her. He felt her hand on his chest, comforting, as if it was he who'd been hurt. Wood was baffled, sated, too drained to think.

They dropped off quickly. Later that night, they woke in each other's arms for a second tasting. And then, just before dawn, there was a third.

He surfaced from sleep. Tamarind's taste was still on his tongue. She shifted beside him, touching his thigh.

"Wood—" She sounded troubled.

"What is it?"

"Will you do something for me?"

"What can I do?"

She whispered in his ear.

"Of course," he said.

But her request was unusual. Unusual for him. He'd never done anything like that with Vadette. He was afraid to ask Tamarind for guidance, so he trusted to guesswork and hoped for the best.

The breeze was still blowing, sprays hissing in darkness. Bunches of pods hung from the boughs—scores of them, and new pods were growing. The Tamarind tree was loaded with fruit, far more, it seemed, than any man could consume.

Wood pulled off the pods in handfuls and crushed them, and as soon as the gluey pulp passed his lips, he reached for more. The words she had spoken, the "something" she wanted— His senses were drowning. The floods of sensation— It was all he could do to swallow them down. His mouth was full to bursting now, and he sucked on the seeds until they were bare.

Then he opened his mouth, and with a shudder and groan, Tamarind's seeds fell into his hands. They were dark and shiny, and blackish-brown. And in every one, he could see his reflection.

All at once, the wind stopped. The hissing ceased, the leaf sprays hung limp. The tree quivered as if something spiteful had hold of its roots. And then, as Wood watched, the pods fell to the ground. More let go, more and still more, rattling and falling until the wilting canopy was empty.

The room was dark. A window was beaded and dripping. All but one candle had guttered out. Wood whispered Tamarind's name, but she didn't respond.

A buoy horn sounded over a hidden reef.

He closed his eyes and drifted back to sleep.

"Wood?" Tray answered.

"I'm at the Plantation," Wood said, "eating lunch. What a night."

"We heard," Tray said.

"Can you join me?"

"I've got a client. You and I should talk. My last session ends at five, if you're free."

"Sure. I need Tamarind's number."

"Let's save that," Tray said. "My office, at five."

Silence.

"Bijou spoke to her," Wood guessed.

"She did. Tamarind had a great time."

"But?"

"At five," Tray said.

When the call ended, Wood paid for his half-eaten meal and left.

"I'm not your therapist," Tray said, "but maybe I can help."

They were in Tray's office, eight feet apart, sunk in two overstuffed chairs.

"What did she say?" Wood asked.

"She enjoyed your company, like Bijou and I do. You're sincere, and you can laugh at yourself. I'm guessing she'd like to be a friend. As a lover—" Tray shook his head. "From what she told Bijou, that's not in the cards."

"Because?"

"She didn't think you were interested in her."

"I had my arms around her all night." Wood's tone was bleak. He was expecting news that would hurt him.

"'He doesn't want to know who I am.' Those were her words."

Wood exhaled.

"Every man's curse," Tray said.

Wood saw the sadness in his eyes. He was speaking as one of the afflicted.

"We can't see beyond ourselves," Tray said. "I hear that from Bijou."

"I had," Wood scowled, "an understanding of love." He looked at his hands as if something had fallen through them. "I did. Really, I did."

"I've glanced at *Unborn Twins*. I'm going to read it. But I think I get the idea."

"My marriage was built around the Sacred Space," Wood said. "Vadette was my other half." His words sounded absurd, but Tray wasn't laughing. The sun was sinking behind him.

"Tell me about that," Tray said.

Wood looked away, finding the place—dark and warm—vacant now, but still alive in his mind. "We were sheltered, protected. One, not two. For five years, the Space kept us together."

"The struggle," Tray said, "that so many men and women go through to align their needs and desires— For you and Vadette, it was no effort at all."

"That's right. It was easy. Effortless."

"That sounds wonderful, Wood. What happened?"

"She wouldn't tell me."

"Vadette decided it was over on her own."

"That's right."

"Why didn't she say, 'I'm unhappy, Wood. The Sacred Space isn't working. Love isn't easy for me. I don't feel like your twin. Let's talk.'"

"I wish I knew."

"Would you have listened to her?" Tray asked.

Wood thought about that. His conviction about the Sacred Space had been strong. In many ways, he'd been as wedded to it as he was to Vadette.

"Maybe not," he said finally.

Wood left Tray's office feeling hollow inside. His thoughts were gloomy, his attention distracted. He let his feet go where they pleased. They took him to the north side of town, where shops were scattered among one-story homes.

He found himself in front of a restaurant with a Chinese name: Hao Zhidao. Through the doorway, it looked more like a theater than a place to eat. At the rear was a proscenium arch with scrolls and droops painted pink and gold. Diners were seated at tables on the thrust stage beneath.

Wood crossed the threshold. On his right, a painting of an orchard hung on the wall. Beneath it was an empty booth with naugahyde seating. He stepped toward it and sat down. Under the proscenium, at the restaurant's rear, were two golden doors. They parted, and a woman passed through.

With a stride measured and calm, the waitress approached. She was small and Asian, a modern girl with a layered bob and turquoise nails. Without a word, she set the menu before him, filled his cup with tea, unfolded the napkin and placed it on his knees.

Wood looked at the menu. "Is there something you'd recommend?"

"Our special tonight," the waitress said. "Sizzling Chicken with Wood Ear."

"Food that talks."

"You taste," she said, "and you listen."

"I'll try it."

The waitress bent at the waist as she wrote. Her smile was fixed, her ideograms small and precise. She had a celestial fragrance, and as she departed, it trailed behind her.

She reappeared ten minutes later, head high, with a steaming plate on a silver tray. She lowered the dish before him, and as the meal snapped and sizzled, she removed his chopsticks from the paper casing.

"Thank you," Wood said. "What's your name?"

"Guava."

"This is a wonderful place," he said, looking around.

Lanterns in bamboo cages hung from the ceiling. There was an orchid beside the cash register and a giant folding fan on the wall above the restaurant's entrance. A green mountain with a winding river was painted on it.

When he'd finished eating, Guava returned with her tray. The check was there, along with a fortune cookie. She extended the tray with a solemn expression.

Wood turned the cookie in his hands. Guava stood sentry, watching. He set his thumbs against the cookie's wings and broke it open.

OUR FIRST LOVE IS SELF LOVE, the fortune said.

3

That night Wood's sleep was troubled. He was in the Sacred Space, but it was like a London aquarium during the Blitz. He was trapped inside, tumbled and drowning while the shelling scattered the gems and cracked the shell. Familiar faces watched from a viewing gallery, immune to the havoc—Tray, Bijou, Tamarind and Vadette.

When he awoke the next morning and drew the curtains, he was relieved to see a blue sky. And when he stepped outside, a golden sun warmed his front. Latin music *plinked* from a neighbor's backyard.

Three blocks to the east was a Cuban market. A sign over the awning read "Buen Sabor" and the tables were loaded. Wood wandered among them, touching the fruits, admiring their colors and fragrance, happy for the respite from his troubling thoughts. The fruits were beautifully arranged. Many of them Wood had never seen before.

A big woman was hunched over a pile, and when she straightened, she caught sight of him and grinned. "Do you like these?" she asked, lifting a fruit. It was green and lumpy and as large as a human head.

Wood stepped toward her. "They're good?" He eyed the fruit in her hands, then grasped another and held it under his nose. It smelled like a citrus. Where the stem had attached, the odor was full; at the opposite end, the perfume was sharp.

"Incredible," the woman replied.

She was in her fifties, Wood guessed. Six feet in sandals, ball-nosed and brassy, with gray hair and capacious breasts.

"You juice it?"

"Section it," she said.

His eyes searched hers. "You have some guidance for me."

She drew back, surprised.

"I'm sorry," he said. "I'm in trouble. Looking for help."

"What an earnest young man." Her brow rumpled, considering. "I don't know you well enough to give you advice. But this fruit would lighten your spirits." She tapped the citrus he held in his hands.

Wood smiled. "Can you tell me what to do with it?"

She seemed charmed by his smile, and goodwill grew like a bubble around them.

"Well—" Her lids fluttered. "Rinse it, then remove the rind—"

Wood nodded, acutely attentive.

The woman laughed. "Walk me home, and I'll show you. We'll take both."

She reached for her purse, but before she could open it, Wood pulled some cash from his pocket and dropped it in the payment basket. He took her citrus, and holding one under each arm, he led the way out from under the awning.

"This way," she pointed. And they started down the street together.

Coincidentally, she explained, her name was Pumelo, like the fruit. She was born in Florida. She'd been trained in addiction recovery and managed a food bank on the Key.

"I didn't know there was one," Wood said.

"There are always people in need."

Her faded tunic was roomy and wrinkled, and her large breasts and buttocks joggled inside. When they reached her flat, Wood followed her into the kitchen.

Pumelo placed the two green soccer balls on the cutting board. "You're going to enjoy this," she said, eyes glittering. "But first," she motioned him into her front room, gesturing at the cushions scattered on the floor, "I want to know more about you."

Wood sat down. Pumelo bound up her woolly locks with a mahogany fork, took a seat across from him and folded her legs beneath her. "Happy chance," she sighed. "What a striking figure you cut." She admired his bouffant and the browned legs that emerged from his shorts. "Well now. Start from the beginning. The little Wood. Who had the pleasure of peeling fruit for *him*?"

"I had to fend for myself," he told her. "My mother was an invalid."

"Oh my."

"She couldn't leave her bed."

"Poor woman," she said. "Poor Wood. A child depends on his mother."

Her candor and empathy made the recounting easier. He told her about his stepfather, about growing up in the oilfields. And when she asked, he explained how he'd come home from school and found his mother dead.

"Poor woman," she said. "Poor Wood." Then she smiled. "But you turned out fine. You've had your pick of the girls, I'll bet."

"I was married," he said. And when Pumelo asked, he explained how he and Vadette had met, why they didn't have children, what their life together was like in the beginning and at the end.

"She didn't just say goodbye," Wood said.

Pumelo looked into his eyes.

"She found a man she liked better," he said.

She leaned forward and touched his hand.

Wood thought of himself as a private person, but in his battered condition, his boundaries were gone. Pumelo seemed genuinely caring. So he let her see his shame and humiliation.

"Poor, poor Wood," she said.

He told her about the Sacred Space, how it had been a heaven for him; and then somehow, without his knowing, it had become less than heaven for Vadette.

"Sometimes," Pumelo nodded, "when our own needs are

urgent, we can't see anything else."

"Was I really that blind? Maybe she felt she had to hide the truth from me."

"Do you think she was lonely?"

Wood considered the idea. "I guess she was."

"That's wonderful," Pumelo said.

"Wonderful?"

"That you can imagine how she felt. I'm proud of you."

"I didn't mean to be cruel," he said.

"I know." Her eyes were moist. "Poor Wood. Poor wife."

He nodded slowly. "Poor wife." It was as if a curtain had been drawn, and he could see through a window he never knew was there.

Pumelo was studying him. Her eyes were deep and misty.

"You really care about me," Wood said.

"I care about everyone. Trouble is our birthright, Wood. None of us escape it. I took a woman to the shelter this morning. The poor dear hasn't a nickel. She's very confused, and there was no one looking out for her. Well—" She patted his knee and rose. "Let's refresh ourselves. Our fruit will do that."

Wood followed her into the kitchen. She washed the two giant citrus and removed their ends with a butcher's knife. Using her stubby fingers, she peeled away the thick rinds and divided each fruit into quarters. Then she pulled the pink sections from their membranes and placed them on a platter. When the job was done, she led him out onto her deck.

They sat together on a bench overlooking the sea. Pumelo

took a glistening section and raised it to Wood's lips. That made him uncomfortable, but she wouldn't be denied. So he let her feed him.

"What do you think?" she asked, wiping his chin with her fingers.

"It's a subtle taste," he said. "Not acid, not sweet. Crisp and clear."

Her eyes met his. She touched his cheek. "I'm a soppy old thing," Pumelo said. "But you can have me, if you like. I won't be disappointed if the answer is no."

The idea was unthinkable. And then, in a moment, it seemed to Wood that it was natural and right. His world, his reality, had changed. It was the perspective of age that he needed, the patience of age, the understanding.

The hem of her tunic was at her thigh. Wood put his hand beneath it. The flesh was warm and expansive. Her eyes were enormous. They saw everything—his simplicity, his mistakes— They were the eyes of a saint, inured to the suffering of others.

"Lonely boy, motherless child," she whispered. "It's so wrong."

Wood embraced her. Her mouth was roomy, her tongue large and smooth. He felt her thighs closing around him. Her pulse was measured and slow, and the throb invaded his chest, mastering his heart, calming it.

She drew back, removed her arms from the tunic and pulled it down, baring her breasts. They were giant globes with bumpy nipples the color of dirt.

"Enjoy them," she said. "Do whatever you like."

Wood eyed them nervously.

She took his hand and placed it on one, shuddering with anticipation.

He struggled to oblige her, but his fingers barely moved. His arousal halted in its tracks.

Wood removed his hand.

"What's the matter?" she asked.

"You're treating me like a child."

"Was it different with your wife?"

"Very different."

"Wrong, so wrong," Pumelo said. And then, "If it's too upsetting, just pretend they aren't there." She stroked his head.

Then Pumelo rose. There was a canvas umbrella with a straw mat beneath. She led Wood to it, and the two knelt together. It was like the shade of a small tree. A green lizard scurried behind a planter with lavender flowers. Pumelo stretched out and raised her arms with a gentle hum, welcoming him back to the earth. Wood planted his palms on the mat and lowered himself.

Her lids quivered like moths. Her body spread, dropping him between the loam of her thighs. It was evening, cool and dark, and he was in an orchard. Scents of humus and dew and sap wafted through the branches, and the trees around him were thick with fruit, loaded with lumpy green soccer balls, enough to feed an army of penitents.

Here on this island, an intimate embrace drew the curtain on a world he had never seen or knew existed. An unsheltered world, open to the elements, with fertile earth and teeming trees and an endless largess of ripe delights.

Wood found a slow rhythm. He was aroused, but his distress was still with him—the shame of being left, along with fresh suspicions about how and why Vadette had turned against him.

"Poor wife, poor Wood," Pumelo chanted in time with his strokes.

His pleasure mounted and so did his pain. Aching for solace, he poured it into her.

"Wrong, so wrong," she said. "So very wrong."

The sap rose. The trees trembled. The boughs drooped as the fruit swelled.

Something was wrong with Pumelo.

At the deep end of his forays, her whole body shook.

Was this how she expressed herself? Was he the cause? He was churning inside, with ardor and sorrow, and as his emotion surged, her shaking became more pronounced—a shudder that persisted for seconds.

Was she feeling his loss, or acting it out?

The whole orchard was quaking now, boughs bent and the fruits enormous, many so heavy they touched the ground. Would he shatter the green world inside her? Her heart was drubbing, faster and faster. She clutched him, pressing him close—

"So wrong," she moaned, "so wrong, so wrong."

All at once, Wood knew.

In this act of love, she wasn't just suffering with him. She was trying to help him look into himself.

"Why?" he whimpered. What had he done?

Pumelo hugged him, and as his peak approached, her shudders wove through him. From deep inside her, sections of crystalline fruit tore loose, their fine inner diamonds clashing together, sunbeam and pink, as fresh as the wind blowing over the sea.

"Alone and empty," she whispered. "Poor boy, poor boy—"

The wealth inside her glittered for him, with woe, not joy.

"You were so wrong," she said.

Her words confused him, but her inflection did not. She was faulting him.

"So very wrong." Her pity had turned from his injuries to the conception of love that he'd spawned. That fruit, too, looked bright and clear, but it was pulled from blighted recesses, loosed from bitter membranes, parted from bitter rinds. The lips cringed and the tongue recoiled. A wrong idea. A conception cruel to two, not one.

"So wrong," she shuddered, "so wrong, so wrong—"

A flood of juice broke over him, diamonds and rhomboids crushed, releasing their scathing bounty as his stung heart clenched. Pumelo was there, clenching with him, sharing the squeeze of wrong and remorse.

The Sacred Space was a lie, Wood thought, and he'd locked himself in it. An enormous gulp, but he swallowed it down.

The orchard dissolved. The imagined night faded to day.

When he opened his eyes, he was on a mat beneath a canvas umbrella. The woman he held seemed frail and small, like a tree whose life had gone into its fruit.

Pumelo slid from beneath him and entered the house.

Wood lay back, her warmth still with him. When he touched his chest, he could feel the scab, but the pain had dulled. His flesh was calm, his nerves were quiet.

He raised himself slowly and stared at the sea. The light was reflected on it, and a lone boat was visible, its sails full of wind, tacking aimlessly over the sunlit water.

"I should have known," Wood said. "There were plenty of signs."

"Such as?" Tray raised his head.

They were at Bijou's house, in the second-floor den, seated across from each other. The windows were open, and a breeze blew through.

"She had tantrums," Wood said. "She broke things."

"What kinds of things?"

"Whatever she could get her hands on. One night she destroyed the dishes."

"That upset you?"

Wood shrugged. "Who cares about dishes."

"When she had a tantrum, did you talk about the reason?"

"Of course."

"You knew she was discontented."

Wood nodded. "I knew, but I didn't take what she said seriously. It didn't seem important."

"Because?"

"The love we had made up for everything."

"If Vadette were here now," Tray said, "would she agree with that?"

"Obviously not. Toward the end, she was taking long walks by herself. She would return with this puzzled look. As if something had happened—she'd seen something or lost something."

Tray nodded. "I finished *Unborn Twins*. Before I read it, I'd been asking myself whether a man like you—a creative man inclined to detach himself from reality—might ask for a special kind of devotion from the woman he loves. Would he use his imagination to see things in her that weren't really there? The novel answered my question."

"You think the Vadette I married was my creation."

Tray cocked his head. "I keep hearing that you didn't know who she was." His gaze turned inward. "We all trick ourselves. Proust railed against 'the botched work of amorous illusion.'"

A knock sounded at the door. It opened and Bijou appeared. "Dinner's in ten." The door closed, and her footfalls faded.

Wood took a breath. "The Sacred Space was more than a story. It was part of our lives. We spoke as if we were in it. And we acted it out."

Tray was surprised. "What did you do?"

The ritual had been a guarded secret, but there was no longer anything to protect. So Wood explained.

Vadette would close the drapes, insuring that no light would penetrate the darkness. He turned off the phones and bolted the bedroom door. Then, while she stripped off the bedding and built a nest on the mattress with sheets and quilting, he went to the bathroom and ran a scalding shower. They stood face to face and undressed each other, and once they were naked, they stepped into the spray together and remained there until they were lathered and dripping. Then they covered each other with coconut oil.

They returned to the darkened bedroom and took their positions in the nest together. Then, using lines he'd written, they described the Space to each other from memory. Its walls were curved, swollen, throbbing and gleaming—a cocoon, frilled and flounced, hung with jewels, seeping with mucous or finned with long-armed stars.

They were strangers at first, senseless bodies floating apart with nodded heads. Then slowly they entered each other's meditation.

Wood reached through the tarry darkness. Her skin was soft and where his fingerpads touched it, guilloche patterns spread. He drew her closer, and she drew him. Closer and closer, until they curled together.

An effortless dance, no leading or following, no give or take. They rolled in a ball, like eels in oil, slicked and jelled, palmed and pressed, molded by love. As their boundaries dissolved, they shivered with pleasure—shivers that printed the darkness with lines that spread like ripples across a pool. And as the ripples thickened, the triumph of the Sacred Space hove into view.

They worshipped at the altar of the final moment: two peaks of pleasure superimposed. Perfect, equal, twin natures aligned and fusing— One sigh, one heave, one buckle, one moan—

And then, there it was: the Sacred Moment.

An infant helpless, quaking with rapture, with love in its heart, love in its soul, love in its bones.

Slowly, slowly, the Moment subsided. The babe blurred and dissolved. The eels parted. Their bodies were human again, discrete; and the living cocoon was blankets and sheets.

Vadette began to sob.

That, too, was part of the ritual. The tears weren't gladness. She sobbed for what they had gained and what they had lost, and she cried for them both. Vadette and the Space were full of mysteries, but this was the deepest.

"Unborn twins," Wood muttered. "A story for fools."

"Or children."

Wood saw the care in Tray's eyes.

"When we're young," Tray said, "we can dream that two really are one."

Wood woke to find a message from Cameron on his phone. "Feeling better? Ready to head home?"

"I like it here," Wood texted back. "I want to stay."

An hour later, Cameron called. The assignment in Cambodia had ended, he said, but he was moving to London and the landlord was giving the place to his brother. "Sorry, man. You've got till Friday and that's it."

Buen Sabor's pink awning flapped in the breeze. Wood ducked beneath it, ambling among the fruit tables, squeezing a mango, touching a fig, pausing beside a pyramid of pale brown ovoids marked "Sapodilla." He took one from the top, feeling its felty skin, weighing it in his palm.

"They're just right," a woman said.

She wore a pink apron. She smiled as she removed limes from a box.

Wood smiled back. "How can you tell?"

"They speak to me," she said.

Wood nodded. He held the sapodilla to his ear, regarding the woman. She was big and solidly built. Her dark eyes were kindly, her hair lopped at the earlobes. About my age, he guessed. "This one's quiet," he said.

"She's shy. She doesn't know you."

Wood lowered the fruit and turned it in the light between them. "She has an unassuming exterior."

The woman laughed, drew a knife from her pocket and

unfolded the blade. She took the brown fruit from him, sliced it, peeled the skin off and handed it back.

Wood bit into the pulp. It was sweet and grainy, with a hint of cinnamon. "Wow."

"They're all grown locally," she scanned the tables around them, "by Cuban immigrants. Guava, grapefruit, cashew, caimito—" She pointed with her knife, recognizing them like children in a schoolyard.

"That's a grapefruit?"

"Mm-hmm."

"It's different than any I've seen," he said.

"Fruit is a blessing from God."

"Really." Wood took another bite of the sapodilla.

"When they're hanging on the branches," she said, "they dream of being eaten."

He raised his brows. "Sacrificing themselves."

"It's no sacrifice," the woman said. "They're trusting and wise." She held up the other half of the sapodilla. "Life has a million ways to reproduce, but the glory goes to the fruit-bearers. They're gift givers. To everyone. Parakeets, monkeys, iguanas—"

"They want us to eat them and poop their seeds out," Wood said.

"So they make themselves fragrant and beautiful," she smiled. "What an idea."

"It's a trick."

"No. It's a natural generosity that hopes for something in return. It's love. They love us, and we love them."

Her words were like music. "What a wonderful thought," he murmured, letting them soak in. "I'll have a few of these." He took a basket and placed four sapodillas in it. "And a papaya."

"Ah— *La fruta suprema*. We're out right now."

"I'm Wood. Let me guess: you're Sapodilla."

"No, I'm Mamey." She folded her knife.

"I used to have one like that."

"Did you?" she grinned.

"You live in the neighborhood?" he asked.

She nodded.

"Maybe you can help me. I'm looking for a place to rent."

Mamey looked surprised. "There's one right around the corner." She pulled a felt pen from her pocket protector, turned over the sapodilla half, and wrote a number on its skin. "How's that for luck?"

As he strolled toward Duval, Wood called the landlord. The apartment was available, and he made an appointment to see it. When he disconnected, he was passing a shrimp shack and a tattoo parlor. A short woman stood in the gap between the two, fingering her phone. Wood recognized the fountain of green hair.

He crossed the street, waving as he approached.

Piña recognized him with a lopsided smile. "Did you get home safely?"

"You frightened me," he admitted. "A lot's happened since then. My view of women has changed."

"Is that good?"

"I think so." He hung his head, duncing himself. "They have lives of their own."

"How about that." Piña scowled at her phone.

"I'm sorry I got out of your car."

She regarded him. "You've got the timing. He was a shithead that night, and he's a shithead this morning."

Wood asked for her number, and she gave it to him.

Piña slid her phone into her pocket. "Back to work." And she disappeared into the tattoo parlor.

The apartment to let was on the top floor of an updated three-story. It had a parking space, a view through one window and was furnished with deco rattan. Wood rented it on the spot.

When he arrived with a load of clothing, he met the tenant with whom he shared the third floor. Their doors faced each other. No sooner had he put the key in his lock, then the door opposite swung open and Mamey stepped out.

He laughed. "I was going to stop by and thank you."

"How do I look?" She was dressed for a date.

"Beautiful." Her outfit was brown and her lips were ruby.

She suggested some local eateries and scenic spots on the Key. "I love Taylor Beach and the leaning pines."

"I want to see that."

"It's best at sundown," she said. "Tomorrow?"

"Thank you. Really."

The next day, Mamey knocked on his door as the sun was setting. She wore a drab shirt and baggy shorts. On the drive there, she talked about herself. Her parents were Cuban exiles and lived on Islamorada. She had been in the Keys all her life. She loved her family, and she wanted one of her own.

"Babies," she said. And then, "Do you think perfect love is possible?"

"I used to," Wood said.

"You've been married."

He nodded. "Technically, I still am."

Taylor Beach was a place of romance. Its leaning pines seemed drunk with it, the needle sprays trembling. They strolled through the trees, passing couples arm in arm. Mamey watched, her eyes on the women. As they reached the shore, what remained of the sun stained the eastern sky pink. The winds had left ripple patterns in the duff. Where the pines ended, a little girl was turning circles with a bottle of soap, freeing bubbles from her wand—iridescent blue, green and yellow. They were lifted by the breeze and borne out to sea.

Wood faced Mamey, trying to see her as she was, unbiased by any need or desire of his own. He caught her hand, and when she squeezed it, his heart went out to her. She seemed so unassuming, so vulnerable.

"There's a jetty," she pointed.

They crossed the sand, clambered onto the rocks and followed the pile out beyond the breaking surf. When they reached the jetty's end, they stood together with the sea all around them. "I'm so happy here," she said.

Without thinking, Wood's lips approached hers. She turned her face, bashful, accepting the kiss on her cheek.

"You're embarrassing me," she muttered. Wood barely heard. Her cheek was smooth as custard, and its colors in the flare of sun were pink and orange. Her scent was subtle, simple and clean, like bread fresh from the oven. It mingled with the taste of a dozen rare spices, all in small traces.

Her dark eyes met his. "I'm still a girl," she said. "The things a woman feels— They're a mystery to me."

"Woman or girl, your warmth is magnetic. You're beautiful, inside and out."

She bowed her head. "My family's Catholic. I'm following the faith. It might surprise you, or amuse you—"

"What?"

She faced him. "I'm a virgin. I'm saving myself for the man I marry."

He nodded slowly, fighting his feelings. For her, love meant sanctity. Did his failure separate them? The loss of the Sacred Space was, after all, a fall from grace.

"Wood—"

Her expression was earnest. She turned her head, and for a moment he imagined it was the sail of a ship coming about, headed away from him.

"Have you ever had a woman as a friend?" she said.

"I'm not sure."

Mamey turned back to him.

"Maybe I need one," Wood said.

"I need a friend too. I'm still learning about love." She laughed. "But I know a lot about fruit."

The cheer in her eyes stopped his breath. Once again, he felt himself the lucky beneficiary of a generous heart.

"Do you like Chinese food?" he asked.

Hao Zhidao was packed, but Guava was on duty, and she treated Wood like an imperial guest. She knelt beside him, conferring and advising on meal selection, and after she set down the steaming plates, she stood by his shoulder and broke open the paper casing, extending the square ends of the chopsticks toward him while Mamey watched.

"Special treatment," Mamey observed as the waitress moved away. And they began to eat.

"You stock guavas," Wood said.

"Whenever we can," Mamey replied. "An austere fruit that needs careful attention. The raw guava is pasty and astringent, and the little seeds are hard as gravel. You juice it or make a gel and bake it in pastry."

"The scent is heavenly," Wood said.

When they'd finished eating, Guava approached with the check on her silver tray, and a fortune—just one.

"What about my guest?" Wood said.

"Her future is known." Guava extended the tray. "It's yours that's in doubt."

Mamey laughed.

Wood removed the cellophane while the two women watched. He stared at the fortune, then read it aloud.

"TO FIND A NEW LIFE, YOU MUST FORGET WHO YOU ARE."

When Wood arrived at Refugio, Piña was at the bar talking to Mango. He ordered blushes. "Put a squirt of pineapple in mine," Piña said. "Where did you get that shirt?" she laughed. He was wearing a blue pajama top.

"I thought you'd like it."

"I do. The ducktail too." She reached up and touched his hair.

While they drank, Piña told him about the tattoos she'd inked that day. Then she began asking questions. Wood told her about the breakup and his move to the Key.

"Stabbed in the heart," Piña said. "I know what that's like."

"It hurts to be left."

"Don't be so dainty." Piña wrinkled her nose. "Two-timing stinks. It's fucked."

He nodded at her assessment.

She studied him. “You’re trapped in there. Aren’t you.”

“Trapped?”

Piña downed the rest of her blush and set the goblet on the bar. “We’re going to open you up.” She motioned him to follow.

They were halfway to the door when the old woman, Auntie, plowed through the crowd. “Coconuts,” Piña warned.

Auntie threw her arms around Wood.

“Leave him alone.” Piña pushed her away.

Auntie elbowed Piña aside and planted a kiss on Wood’s mouth. “My baby.”

Wood wiped his lips. “You’re confused.”

“I’m the one you want,” Auntie exclaimed.

“You witch.” Piña was prying Wood loose, but Auntie kept hold of one arm.

With her free hand, the old woman fished a pen from her purse and scrawled a phone number on his palm.

Wood turned to Piña when they reached the sidewalk. “Who the hell is she?”

“Auntie Coco,” Piña shook her head. “You don’t need that.”

“I’ll say I don’t.” He put his thumb to his palm, but the number wouldn’t rub out.

“Always looking for a guy to keep her pump primed.”

Piña grabbed Wood’s arm and pulled him into an alley. “Here,” she opened her purse, drew a pipe out and lit it. “Try this.”

“What is it?”

"Try it," she insisted.

Wood did, and the lift-off was instant.

"Powerful," he said.

"Stubby's stuff," she muttered.

"Who's that?"

"My ex. I loved him, but I hate him now. He was screwing around, like Vadette."

Wood remembered her plea for an escort to her car. "Is he bothering you?"

Piña nodded. "He's got a gun." She raised her thumb and forefinger, with an inch between. "A black one with a little nose." She drew on the pipe, put it back in her purse and motioned. "Let's go."

Duval was mobbed. A squadron of honking scooters tore down it, panicking tourists in a crosswalk and the chickens crossing with them. They passed a man supported by two women, his feet wobbling behind. A crowd had gathered at the Truman intersection. Piña slowed, and the two of them watched as the fire squad carried out an alligator someone had left in a belle époque guesthouse.

Past the fire truck, Piña halted before a stairway. She turned and patted Wood's chest. "This is our place."

She led him into the stairwell and up three floors.

As they reached the rooftop, Wood saw people milling before a bar, half of them unclothed. Beyond the bar, beneath potted palms and canvas umbrellas, couples were dancing naked in the humid night air.

He looked at Piña and shook his head.

She pushed him toward a doorway. "In there."

The changing alcove was like a locker room. Men were removing their clothes or putting them on while the floor tipped beneath them. "I'm high," he warned, unsure if anyone heard. *Stupid*, he thought, unbuttoning his shirt. He slid off his shorts and his briefs, and hung his things on a hook. Then he stepped back through the doorway, steeling himself.

Piña was exiting a changing room on the other side of the bar. Her naked body was all tight curves and sharp edges. The ink he'd seen on her arm and shoulder was part of a larger tattoo that crossed her breasts, wove over her hips and belly, and wound down both thighs.

"Like my jungle?" Piña turned. "I did the drawing."

Lianas and serpents writhed over her back. Between her hips, a snake's head looked out, eyes glaring, its forked tongue curling over her buttocks.

"What are you hiding?" She laughed and caught his wrist, pulling his hand away from his groin. "Let's dance."

She dragged him past the DJ, onto the roof deck. The music was latin, frenzied, absurdly cheery. Piña began to shake. Wood ducked his head and shuffled his feet, shifting his hands before him, as if he was waving at someone he didn't want to meet. She faced him, wide-eyed, tossing her head, making her green fountain thrash. Then she squinted at him and wrinkled her nose.

Wood looked away. He could laugh at himself, but his life

had always been private. He was feeling now how private it was. Could Piña hear his thoughts? She was twirling against him, poking his middle, slapping his rump.

Laughter reached him. Dancers and people seated at tables were turning to watch. Piña was laughing too, still twirling, pointing at him at each rotation. As she gyrated past a table, she grabbed a drink, and as she came around, she threw it in his face.

Wood's reserve burst. He felt the drink dripping down his chin. It was tropical, fruity; he tasted the sweetness, and in a flash, with the laughing eyes on him, he let himself go, jerking his hips and flailing his limbs to the zany music. His head bobbed, his tongue wagged—he was a child again, silly and witless, flinging his body around.

Piña collapsed in his arms. "Let's eat," she said.

They dressed and descended the stairs. She paused on the first-floor landing and pulled out her pipe, and they smoked what was left. When they reached the street, it was heaving like a cruise ship in a tempest.

Piña led the way down Duval to a Cuban place with "Papalote" over the door. They found an empty spot on the bench before one of three long tables. All the walls were sky blue, and a giant kite was painted at the rear, with its tail and string trailing.

"Where are the waiters?" Wood wondered.

Piña shook her head.

And the menus?

"There aren't any," she said.

The people seated, Wood realized, were all drinking pink blushes. And they were all staring at him and Piña.

"Go to the kitchen," she said. "Tell the cooks what we want."

Wood rose and elbowed his way to the rear. Vats were bubbling on the burners, and large pans of food steamed on racks. Were the cooks on drugs? They were jabbering to each other, but the jabber sounded like baby talk. Wood tried to make himself heard, but what came out was baby talk too. He shouted and pointed at the food.

One of the cooks slopped big portions on a pair of red plates, and Wood carried them out of the kitchen. As he approached, he saw a man slide beside Piña. She was talking loudly and gesturing, and Wood could hear what she was saying.

She was telling the man that she and Wood were going to have sex. She was explaining the things she was going to do, and the things she would have Wood do to her. Everyone at the table was listening. One of them spotted him and hooted. As he set a plate down in front of Piña, she removed her shoe and threw it at the hooter. The man beside her, seeing an opening, pinched her breast. Piña scooped up a handful of refried beans and smeared his face. Wood turned his plate over, dumping its contents on the man's head.

People at the other tables were standing. Cries, catcalls, and then the food was flying. As Wood pulled Piña to her feet, the cooks exited the kitchen with vats and pans, throwing fistfuls at the diners. Was any of this really happening? Wood grabbed Piña and hurried her toward the door. Covered in food, they piled into a pink cab.

"Where to?" the driver asked.

"Stock Island," Piña said.

The cab headed east, zooming around bends and through red lights. Old Town vanished, strip malls and chain stores flew past. Then, through the bouncing window, Wood saw boats canted together, docked and weatherworn, with rickety cabins and hobbled booms. The cab crossed Cow Key Bridge, skirting hills of chains and rotting nets. Trucks without tires, suspended on blocks; shacks falling off their foundations; then they were winding through a maze of house trailers.

"Home?" Wood said.

Piña eyed him. "A storm brought me."

Everything here was broken, coming apart.

Piña shrieked, and the cab halted.

She piled out and Wood followed, seeing a derelict trailer, imagining a hurricane had dropped it there with Piña inside.

"Quiet," a man barked from a nearby shack.

"Eat shit," Piña yelled.

Then they were past the door, edging through the cramped space. Dirty dishes filled the sink. Piña parted the damp garments that hung from a makeshift line and led Wood to the rear, stopping before a bed littered with clothing.

Wood grabbed a broom handle to steady himself, seeing

the drawing over the bed. Two giant reptiles twisted together in a web of snakes and vines, like the jungle that covered Piña's body. "Gators."

"Crocs," she corrected.

"Fighting."

"Screwing," she said.

One of the crocs had a heart between its jaws.

Piña reloaded her pipe and they traded tokes, then she removed her food-spattered clothes, helped Wood strip off his, pushed the bed mess onto the floor and fell onto the mattress with him.

"Give me that," she said, grabbing his groin.

Wood giggled, fending her off. Something hard dug at his back. He rolled onto his hip, found a shoe and tossed it aside.

"I'm going to bite you, cut you," Piña said. "Make you bleed."

Her claws scratched his ribs. The stud in her lower lip snagged his chin. "You want some Piña?"

Wood slid his hand up her thigh. "I do."

Piña closed her jaw on his shoulder. The pain was intense.

"I'm going to take you apart," she said. There was blood on her lips.

Wood put his hands to her throat, raising himself, looking down at the fountain of hair. He lowered his face into the spray, breathing her scent, feeling the green shaking around him as Piña tried to free herself.

"Get down here," she gasped.

The tattoo of snakes and lianas crept from her limbs and

encircled his. They were binding him, pulling him down, down to where mold furred the roots and grubs squirmed in the sweating soil. Gnats bit his face, green blades parted. Amid a compass of leaves, he could see the barrel-shaped fruit standing on end. Its skin was spiny, hard to handle.

"In the jungle," she said, "we use this."

Piña raised her fist. It gripped a tarnished machete.

"Hack the stalk," she said.

She swung, and the machete hissed through the air. Wood recoiled.

"Hack," she rasped, swinging again.

With a grunt, the fruit came loose. "Grab on," Piña cried. Wood made a fist around hers, and the next hack cut away the fruit's waxy top. Together, they trimmed its bottom and sides.

"Worth the effort?"

"Oh yeah," Piña said. "You'll see."

A fierce chop split the barrel in two, and then they were huffing together, notching and sawing, making broad slices.

The fruit was as unsubtle inside as out. The pulp was fibrous and pitted. There was juice everywhere. Finally the slippery sections were ready.

"Let's feed," she said, closing her eyes.

Wood pushed the fruit into her gaping mouth. She chewed, she swooned. His mind swam, his saliva flowing.

"Open," she croaked, "open!"

He spread his jaws, and she forced a dripping slice between. Coarse, raw—

The acid tang kerfed his tongue and plugged his nose. The crushed pulp slopped from his jowls, drooling over his chin. Piña, Piña— She was crunching and sweetness and irrepressible juice.

The philodendrons shook, the parrots shrieked. The earth was heaving, and all its orchids and beaked heliconias mouthed along. Sweeping palms, fanning ferns; leaves giant and heart-shaped, waving like elephant ears. With the ginger heads, with the fingering fronds and twitching blades, Wood shook and shook.

Slowly the shaking ended.

The closeness and dimness dissolved. Above, the jungle canopy cracked. Wood felt the wind and saw the sun.

He lay on the jungle floor caked with loam, sticky and stiff, body crawling with flies. Around him, palms were uprooted. The plants were rags, stalks snapped, seedheads dashed, vines in knots. It was fading, but he could still hear it—the roar of the hurricane that had come and gone.

He emerged from oblivion slowly, sensation returning. His leg was bound. Something choked him, circling his neck. Wood moved his arm to feel beneath him, but he had no hand. Had he lost it? Had it fallen asleep? Springs squealed as he shifted, turning onto his hip.

Light shone through a broken window. He was tangled in

the sheets on Pina's bed. He pulled the linen from his throat and raised his head. Alone, in her trailer. She had scraped the food off his shirt and shorts, and draped them over a stool.

Wood used her leaky shower to wash himself. There were teeth marks on his chest and shoulder, and a gash in his hip was crusted with blood. As he dressed, he scanned the drawings pinned to walls and ceiling. Writhing foliage, swollen fruit, beady-eyed reptiles. Over the bed, the two crocs mated in a nest of snakes.

He pulled his phone from his pocket to call for a ride and saw a photo Piña had sent him an hour before. He was sleeping, tangled in the sheets. A shin was visible, the hand from one arm, biceps from the other. The linen was bound round his neck, and his head looked detached. It was like a bomb had gone off and scattered his parts.

"Wide open," the caption read.

That afternoon, Mamey knocked on Wood's door. She had made a fruit platter of caimitos and figs, and she had a package wrapped in shiny paper and ribbons. Wood removed the wrapping. It was a leather-bound notebook with blank pages and a cornucopia carved on the cover.

"A logbook," she said.

He touched the horn of plenty. It had been four days since he'd moved his things, with some forwarded mail, from

Cameron's place. He had stood by the window of his new apartment and opened the letter from his publisher. The meager check had driven him back to his computer, but when he reread his notes for the *Unborn Twins* sequel, he knew it was hopeless.

"I'm changing," Wood said. He met Mamey's gaze. "Things are happening to me."

She nodded. "You should write them down."

"Thanks," he said, humbled by the gift. "I will."

After she'd left, he sat at the kitchen table, opened the log to the first page and entered the date. Then he recounted what had happened with Piña.

In the days that followed, Wood recorded the events that led to his flight to Key West and what had happened since his arrival. Along with the events, he set down his thoughts about his failed marriage. How deep was his blindness? How long had Vadette been forlorn? Did the trip to Mazatlán turn her into a scorpion, or had the demon always been with them, lurking in the shadow of his Fabergé egg?

At the end of the week, an envelope arrived by overnight mail. It was from a law firm in L.A. Wood waited until Mamey returned from work and they opened it together. Inside were divorce papers. That night at 4 a.m., Wood rose from sleep. He'd been dreaming that he was with Vadette, speaking his heart to her, and the words were still fresh. He grabbed the logbook and transcribed them.

"In my way, my childish way, I loved you. I still do. Those feelings, those memories will never be erased. Forgive me,

Vadette. The Space was the best I could do. If I'd been a different man—a better one, a smarter one—I might have seen who you were, understood what you needed. I might have given you a real love—the love you deserve."

As he finished, the tangle of feelings about the man in L.A. returned.

Wood went back to sleep, and when he rose the next morning he transferred what he'd written to a blank sheet of paper. He knocked on Mamey's door and had her read it.

"I think you should send it to her," she said.

Wood clipped it to the divorce papers. The two of them had breakfast and then walked to the courthouse. Wood signed the documents in front of a notary. After the notary had used his stamp, Wood felt the embossing with his fingers, imagining she might do the same. Then he posted the papers.

4

Tray answered the door in shorts and a t-shirt, with a book in his hand.

"Bijou's on her way," he said. "She's getting take-out."

He led Wood through the house, out onto the patio, and they sat at a weathered table. The sun was setting over Tray's shoulder.

"What are you reading?" Wood asked.

"Economic theory. It helps me relax. I had a difficult day."

Wood could see the strain in his eyes.

"I advise the court on domestic assault cases," Tray said. "I was questioning a guy going to trial. He blew up at me, and they had to restrain him. The whole week's been like that. Bijou's taken a lot."

"Bijou too?"

"We're both in the 'help' business," Tray said, "but she helps more than I do. She helps her patients at the clinic, and she helps the doctors. And when she's done at the clinic, she has to help me. She's a nurse at work, and a nurse at home. I can't leave anything in the office. I bring it all back."

"That would be hard."

"You have no idea," Tray said. "People are so fucked up."

"She has her faith."

Tray looked confused.

"She wears that giant crucifix," Wood said.

"It belonged to her grandmother. Bijou's religion is us."

She arrived a few minutes later with a sack full of take-out from Hao Zhidao. Tray carried plates to the patio and they filled them from the paper cartons.

"Great food," Wood said.

Tray nodded. "The best."

"We ate there our first night together." Bijou licked her fingers.

"I've got news," Wood said. "I'm out of the Sacred Space. Opening my eyes to the world. Seeing it for the first time."

Bijou's face brightened. "That's so good to hear."

Wood explained how he'd met Pumelo and Piña, and how the encounters had changed his perspective. Then he told them about Mamey and the log book, and the note he'd written to Vadette.

Tray nodded, considering as he ate, saying nothing. Finally, as they reached the end of the meal, he eyed Wood directly.

"Some important things to keep in mind. This new world you're entering—" He put down his chopsticks. "It doesn't work like the Sacred Space. You don't have a twin. And things don't happen automatically, without effort."

"I'm listening," Wood said.

"People have to depend on each other." He glanced at the book on the table. "In commerce, there's the 'invisible hand.' You've heard that expression?"

Wood shook his head.

"At a farmer's market," Tray explained, "the growers price their produce, and the buyers choose what to buy. There's competition, and through self-interest, it all works out. In fact, the growers and buyers are *giving* to each other, but no one understands what they're doing. That's the 'invisible hand.'

"In matters of the heart, no hand exists. Self-interest isn't enough, and if people apply accounting rules to love, it's destructive. We have to keep a spirit of generosity in our thoughts and feelings."

Wood nodded. "I like what you're saying."

Bijou put her arm through Tray's.

"'Generosity' has a wonderful ring to it," Tray went on. "But it's hard. You have to ignore yourself. Your own needs, your own desires. Your concern has to be for someone else in order to give."

The words hung in the air. Wood sat in silence, considering them.

After a minute, Bijou fished in the paper bag. She removed a fortune cookie and handed it to Wood.

He looked at her, puzzled.

"There's only one," she said.

Wood removed the cellophane and cracked the cookie open.

"FATE FAVORS THE FEARLESS," he read.

They rose together, facing the sea. The sun was down.

When the dishes were bussed, Bijou suggested they lighten up, so they headed for Duval.

At a cigar store, Tray bought a stogie. Wood found a straw peon's hat and wore it knocked back on his head. The three laughed and sang as they walked. Tray was greeted by locals. One smiled, another waved, "Hey Doc." As they turned up Duval, the sidewalks were swarming. An old black Bahamian rode by on a giant tricycle, ringing his bells and flashing his lights. Two drunk women had removed their tops and were showing off their breasts. Beside the pharmacy, a man dressed like a Cape Cod yachtsman was greeting tourists. He wore a tie of transparent vinyl, and there were fish in it, with an aerator, gravel and aquatic plants. "Here come the tall girls," Tray said. A gang of seven-foot drag queens approached, on their way to work.

As they passed the Plantation, Wood noticed a woman seated with a small group at one of the outdoor tables. She was speaking loudly, waving her arms, addressing them all. Wood raised his hat to her and circled it over his head. She noticed, but turned away. Wood stepped toward her. Tray and Bijou followed.

As he drew near, the woman faced him, lifting her chin, about to object.

Wood bowed. "I want to give you something," he said, spreading his hands.

She laughed and her challenge dissolved.

"You can start with a drink," she said. She nodded to Tray and Bijou and motioned them to a pair of empty chairs. Wood sat beside her.

A waiter approached. "Four blushes," Wood said.

The woman's hair was orange, and falcate locks framed her face.

"You're Squash," Wood guessed.

"Close. My given name's Calabaza. People call me 'Callie,' but I answer to 'Pumpkin' too."

"I'm Wood. I've been a failure with women."

"Thanks," Callie said. "It helps to know."

"I have to learn how to give."

"That's not so hard."

"It is for me," he said. "My instincts are wrong."

She studied his face, the width of his shoulders and his western shirt. It had smile pockets with arrowhead tacks, and she hooked her finger in one and pulled him closer.

"If feelings and actions don't come naturally, you can always pretend." Callie licked her lips. They were painted burgundy and she had a diastema.

"Pretend?"

"That's what I do. I'm an actress." She pointed down the street. "My play opens night after next." She took Wood's hat and put it on her head.

"I can't act," he said.

"Everyone acts." She clasped his arm. "What makes you think you're not acting right now?"

A dozen tourists passed wearing "Ghost Hunt" tank tops. A homeless man appeared in traffic, wheeling his shopping cart like he was driving a car.

Wood leaned closer, as if he was going to share a secret. "You're the most desirable woman on the Key."

Her eyes sparkled beneath the hat brim. "In the world," she said.

"In the world," Wood nodded. He combed his lower lip with his teeth, as if he was trying to restrain himself. "You've been married?"

"No." Callie's tone darkened. "And I may never be."

Her hand was still on his arm, and Wood felt her nails dig in. She put her lips to his ear. "I need a special man," she whispered. "Very special."

Wood covered her hand with his own. "Maybe it's me."

After they'd downed their blushes, Tray and Bijou departed. A few minutes later, the others in Callie's party did the same.

"Long day," she said. "Hours of rehearsals." She drew back from the table. "Time for bed." Through a gap in her blouse, her breast appeared.

"Can I come with you?" Wood asked.

She regarded him. Then she stood, and Wood saw how much of her there was.

Callie waved at a bicycle rickshaw driver. "If you like."

The apartment had half-a-dozen levels, all painted in pastels and edged with Christmas tree lights. "It belongs to a trans man who's on holiday in Paris," Callie said. "I'm here through the run of our show."

She handed him the script and some publicity photos, then she performed one scene and another, traipsing before him, turning, gesturing, posing and freezing. She paused to light a bubbler, passed it to him and continued her exhibition. Wood applauded after each scene. During the last, Callie removed her shoes and unbuttoned her dress.

As her naked body appeared, Wood smiled and hid his face, like a child caught with a stolen treat. Callie grabbed his hand and led him up a half-flight of stairs, the colored lights blinking around them. There was a loft, dim as a cavern, with a platform bed suspended waist-high.

She began to undress him. "I like these," she murmured, palming his pecs and biceps. When she'd removed his pants, she admired his narrow hips. Wood didn't speak. He smiled, trying to look confident, but he was anything but.

"You're going to be someone you're not," Callie said.

"Playing a part."

"Three parts," she said.

"Three?"

"You're going to give Callie what she wants, aren't you?"

Wood nodded.

"I want to sleep with three different men and have an orgasm with each."

"I'll do my best."

"I'm the director. You'll do what I say. You can't eat Pumpkin raw. You have to give her special attention."

They climbed onto the bed together.

"Lie on your back," Callie said. "I'll explain my scenario."

Wood did as she asked.

"Our heroine is an alluring woman—smart, stylish, with her own special angle on life. Many men desire her. She can take her pick, but her tastes vary from day to day. Instead of restricting her affections to one, our script gives her three lovers. The Cool Guy. The Femboy. And the Virgin. She'll get love from each in a different way.

"First," she stretched beside him, "the Cool Guy. All set? Oh my. You are."

She pulled Wood over her. "You're musclebound. You have giant shoulders, a calculated stubble, and you wear cheap cologne. You're on stage now, Wood. That's right. Play your part, but hold your fire. Don't forget, it's a three-act play.

"A man like you doesn't worry about being tender. Sex, physical sex—that's what women are for. Other than that, they're not worth the grief. Sex is your language. It breathes from your pores. You're a silent man. I cling, I listen for a few words to slip. But there is only the charge of your breath. Is your blade ready?"

Wood slowed, uncertain.

"You can't open your Pumpkin without one," she whispered. "It's a prop, Wood. Stay with me." Her voice turned shrill, tremulous. "You're hard as steel and razor sharp. Your grip is firm. I can't get away. My roundness, my firmness fills your hands. With one, you lift me from the earth, feeling my weight. With the other, you thump my rind with your blade. I'm hollow inside."

What did she want him to do?

"You're a brute," Callie said. "You have something to prove. With one blow, you're going to chop me in two. Fill your chest now. Draw back your blade."

He followed her direction.

"Split her," Callie cried. "Set Pumpkin free."

Wood didn't move.

"Cool Guy," she laughed, "you're losing your cool. Pumpkin's no bonbon. Her pulp isn't soft. She's big and she's tough—maybe tougher than you. Let's try again."

Wood took a breath, reared back and swung.

With a hollow groan, the large fruit split open, its slabby rind glistening on either side. The orange cavity yawned before him, bristling with seeds, its hanging brains shaking. No mush, no seeping; no silence or turning of cheeks. The halved pieces rocked on the shifting mattress, large and gutty, pressure relieved.

"Nicely done," Callie sighed. "Exit stage left."

"Take five," he suggested.

"There's no time," she said. "Your next part is waiting in the wings. The Femboy."

"I'm effeminate?"

"Barely a man," she said. "When you reach center stage, you find the Cool Guy has hacked me to pieces. You're gentle, sensing— You gather me up."

"I'm not sure I can play this part."

"A gift, for Callie."

"I'll try."

"Sweet man." She stroked his temple. "You adore feminine things. Your mind is filled with strange fancies, elaborate ways to honor your love, to pay court to her charms. These thoughts frighten you, but you can't put them aside. Your secret dream is to be a woman.

"What are you doing with my hand mirror, Wood? I found it under your pillow. You took it from my vanity. Weeks ago. How many times have you looked in the glass, imagining you could see my face? The image has faded. The cruel silver is a pool of Narcissus, and a fool's face is reflected—a face you loathe, with painted lips and powdered cheeks.

"Fiddle your fingers," Callie directed. "Mincing steps. Mincing, mincing—"

Wood did his best to play along.

"You're so sensitive," she whispered.

"It's time to groom me. Use your fingers as combs. Pull my strings, lift my mush, remove my seeds— A kiss for the tangle and you set it aside. Nothing pleases you more than to manicure my pulp."

Wood felt her trembling. Was this what she wanted?

Callie circled him with her arms. "Fingers touch my rigid

stem. Fingers touch my blossom end. My flesh is cut into cubes and groomed, and careful fingers arrange me." She guided his hand.

"Spread me on the pan. Raise me with care. The oven door opens, and I feel the heat. Sliding, I'm sliding, sizzling, sweating— The heat closes around me."

Callie shuddered and softened. Act Two had ended.

"How was I?" he asked.

"Perfect," she sighed. "To me, it was all very real."

"Act Three?"

Callie nodded. "The Virgin. Here come your directions.

"You're under a cloud—pensive, moody—and you're always aroused. But a woman's passion— You know nothing about it. You try to imagine— But the overused images don't get you far. Don't worry. It's our secret.

"Of all the women who've fed your fantasies, we know who you'd choose. On your back, Wood. Lie on your back."

He did as she asked.

"Tonight is the night," Callie said. "Your dream will come true.

"Kiss me, kiss me. Not my lips. My shoulder, my neck.

"Don't touch me. Just lay still. Put your arms by your sides and close your eyes. Let me manage this. I know what to do.

"There now— Don't worry. Try to be calm. We're not in a hurry. My god—"

Wood heard Callie gasp.

"You're so big," she said.

Callie settled herself and began to move.

"Are you liking that?" she asked. "Yes, yes, I'm doing fine. Already tingling, crisping, smoking— There were two skilled men before you. The oven's on and I'm very close."

Was the mattress ticking, or was it a hidden timer? Wood jumped when the alarm went off. Callie jumped too. And then she was shaking and shrilling and singeing his face. The oven door opened, and a glory of broiled squash appeared. A great serving of Pumpkin, orange and steaming.

"There it is," Callie sighed.

The Virgin's eyes stared, amazed, disbelieving. But Wood's role had ended. The drama was over. "Go on now," she whispered. "I'm yours to eat."

Wood inhaled her scent, then took a taste. The pulp was toothsome and soft—thanks, perhaps, to the three chefs who'd prepared it. There was little to call sweet. It was all sun and dirt, fiber and heat. He chewed slowly, exploring, finding new odors, new tastes, discovering a deeper woman. Deeper than he'd ever imagined, even with Vadette. By playing three roles, he'd seen three different faces of Callie, all needing love, all wanting what he could give, in their own way. The discovery brought tears to his eyes.

"I know," Callie put her cheek to his. "I know."

They dropped off to sleep together.

Late in the night, Callie drew him close. "I'm horribly busy. Pretending's my life. But—" She sighed and kissed him warmly. "I'll make time for you, if you like."

Old Town was little more than a mile across, so bicycles were popular. Wood thought he might like one, and there was a shop a few blocks away. It was Mamey's day off, so he invited her along. "Love to," she said. "A woman who works there is a friend of mine. And I need your help."

The help had to do with a man she'd met. They talked as they walked.

"He's handsome and smart," Mamey told him, "and he has an odd sense of humor. When I'm with him, I laugh and laugh. He's got a good job and he's very determined. And he's Catholic, which matters to me. But—"

Wood peered at her.

"I'm not sure if it's love," she said.

"You feel helpless?" he asked. "Confused, crazy, out of control?"

She frowned. "Was it like that with Vadette?"

Wood nodded.

"It's not always that way. Is it?"

"I don't know," he shrugged. "The life I'm in now has different rules. I was with a woman last night—an actress. She's amazing. But she scares me."

"That's not good, is it?"

Wood gave her a baffled look.

"You're no help at all," she elbowed his side.

As they entered the shop, Mamey waved, and a young woman stepped from behind the counter. She had cinnamon hair. Her eyes were bright and her lips unpainted. She embraced Mamey.

The woman looked familiar to Wood. The skin of her face was velvety in places, soft with peach fuzz—below her ears, around her lips, at the edge of her cheek.

"My friend Wood," Mamey introduced him. "This is Sapodilla."

"Of course," he said. "Glad to meet you."

"He wants a bike," Mamey said.

"Not a racer," Wood explained. "A bike like the one I had when I was a kid."

Sapodilla fingered the black seeds of her vest. She turned, chewing her gum, and her whistle earrings swung on their chains. "To find our happiness," she motioned, "sometimes we have to look back."

They found a used bike, blue with big tires, that Wood thought was right.

Callie got Wood a seat at her opening, a drama of spurned love with a bombastic part that fit her well. As she crossed the stage, a spotlight followed, enlarging her moods and her windy expressions.

They met at 11 p.m. at Directement, a French restaurant

with a drag show upstairs. Callie wore spiked heels and a black lace dress with leather shoulders. Wood dressed down, in pipe-leg jeans, a white tee and a vaquero jacket. She was in a festive mood. Actors from the troupe were with her. She introduced Wood as her "catch" and made a show of spoiling him. They hooted and Callie grinned with her big painted lips.

Two minutes after they entered her apartment, they were naked on the bed in the loft.

"Another three acts?"

"No. Just one. You're a doctor," she said. "An obstetrician.

"You have an unusual patient. She had sex with three men, and she's carrying a child from each. Triplets. A tricky delivery. The three men are gone. Who can she trust? You, Doctor Wood. She trusts you completely.

"Alright now," Callie exhaled. "The lights are bright. I'm in the stirrups." She gripped his shoulders. "I can't do this without you."

Wood circled her middle.

"It's strange," Callie said. "I'm thinking, 'What a terrible thing to go through,' but there's nothing I want more in the world." She closed her eyes. "I'm ready. Put your forceps inside me."

Wood had no knowledge of obstetrics, but he did his best to pretend. As the procedure advanced, Callie thrashed her head and arched her back. "I've got hold of one," he said finally.

She shuddered and moaned. "A girl?"

He drew out. "No. It's a boy."

"What does he look like?"

"He's perfect," Wood said. "Shall I—"

"Yes, yes."

Wood returned to his task. The second came as easily as the first. This one was a girl. The third was huddled in a recess, and he had to go deeper. Callie clawed his back. Spasms shook her. "Almost," he whispered.

"My baby, my baby," Callie cried.

"Here it comes," he gasped. "Another boy."

He held Callie tightly until her convulsions subsided.

When she'd calmed, he put the three in her arms. "They're beautiful," she said. "And they need me so much."

Serene and blissful, the five fell asleep.

Hours later, Wood heard Callie stirring. She was seated on the bed with a drink in her hand. The odor of whiskey reached him.

When he rose on his elbow, she passed him the glass.

"Can I tell you a story?" Callie said.

She sounded sad. He sat up.

"Once upon a time, a sunny girl lived in a farm town in Indiana. Sunny, sincere and hard-working. Her boyfriend was on the football team. In their senior year, they got engaged. They were accepted to the same university. One morning, she felt a pain." Callie put her hand on her abdomen. "It was ovarian cancer.

"They took her insides. She didn't graduate. She never went to college. The boy she loved married someone else."

Wood felt her grief in the space between them. He leaned toward her, drawing it inside him. His brow touched hers.

"She worked in diners and strip joints and found her way into acting. It's right for her. Pretending. She'll never have children. Without pills, she wouldn't have breasts."

Her words echoed in the close space. Below, the Christmas lights blinked like a view of some distant metropolis.

"To give, Wood. That's what she wanted. More than anything."

They finished the whiskey and lay back down. Wood held her close.

Through the gulf of dream, later that night, an ominous rattle reached him. A hand gloved in latex was shaking the seeds in a dry bean pod. Through the darkness, he could see a giant pumpkin turning. Its shell had been crushed, its insides destroyed. No longer a nest lined with fertile goop, what remained was an arid cavity hung with strings of scar tissue and a few withered seeds—a void where the warm soul of femininity had been cut out.

The dream woke him. He descended the loft, finding his way to the bathroom. He was facing the toilet when a tremor shook him. Instead of urine, a dollop of semen emerged. *What's happening to me?* he thought.

Had he lost control of his body? Or was it a positive sign?

The night had been Callie's. He had delivered her joys and borne her pain without thinking of himself.

The next day Bijou called. Tray was out of town at a conference. "I'm thinking of cooking dinner," she said.

"You're always feeding me," Wood replied. "I'm taking you out."

He picked Ten One Five, a restaurant in a converted Victorian residence on upper Duval.

Once they were seated, Bijou perused the menu. "What happened with the actress?"

"A lot." Wood didn't know how much to share or where to start.

"High drama?"

"Bigger than life. I'm trying to sort out what happened."

"You were intimate," Bijou guessed.

"I was closer to her than I've been to any woman. Even my wife."

Bijou regarded him. "A relationship."

"That's what I'm trying to sort out. She was so brave with me. She just held her breath and jumped. The things she shared—" Wood sighed. "She's survived some terrible trials. My heart aches for her. But love is more than empathy."

"Love can take a while," Bijou said.

"How long did it take for you and Tray?"

"Ten minutes."

"I'm trying to forget how it was when I met Vadette. But

those emotions, deep, spontaneous— They weren't there with Callie."

Bijou pursed her lips, feeling perhaps, Wood thought, some sympathy for the actress. "Do you ever think about kids?" he asked.

"All the time," she said. "I'd have three or four with Tray. He'd make a great dad." She set the menu aside. "I wish he felt the same way."

"There's no rush."

Bijou shook her head. "It's been six years. We've talked about getting married, but I'm still waiting."

"You're patient," he said.

Her gaze softened. "Tray's worth the wait. You understand. You appreciate him."

"I do," he nodded.

"When I'm low, I always come back to the same thing: Tray has an innate nobility. He cares about people, really cares; and he cares about me. He won't let what we have slip away."

"You have faith in him," Wood said.

"I have faith."

Once they'd ordered, she excused herself. While she was gone, Wood checked his phone. There were texts from Callie, Mamey and Piña. He replied to Callie first. "Thinking of you," he said. He was texting Piña when Bijou returned.

The waiter appeared with wine.

"The women here," Wood said, "are bringing me back to life."

"You've got a lot to offer." She raised her glass between them. "You're sharp, you're serious, you're searching for the truth. And you've got that cowboy charm."

"You were upset about what happened with Tamarind," he said.

"I was. But I know you better now. You're a good man."

"Thanks," he said softly. With Bijou, it wasn't the fruit that set her apart; it was her umbrella of leaves. Around her was a big shady tree with branches that reached the ground.

"For so long," he said, "there was only Vadette. Now—"

"Listen to your heart," she said. "You don't need them all. One is enough. You'll know when you've found her."

Wood had his doubts. His judgment was faulty, and his marriage was proof. "I hope you're right."

When they'd finished eating, the waiter brought the check.

"Let me help," Bijou said.

"My privilege." Wood reached for his wallet.

"It's an expensive place."

He laughed. "You look worried."

"I am, a little. It's none of my business, but—"

"What?"

"Are you alright, financially?"

"I get royalties from my novel."

"How long will that last?"

"Please," he said. "What time is it?"

Bijou checked. "I'm late. It was wonderful, Wood. Alright," she stood. "I'm going." And she hurried away.

Wood eyed the check and began counting out bills. He heard footfalls, and the chair across from him creaked. He thought Bijou had returned, but when he raised his head, he saw Auntie Coco.

"You again." Wood shook his head.

"Why haven't you called?" Auntie's tone was mournful. Her hair was ratty and her features were bloated.

"You've got the wrong idea."

"No, dear boy," Auntie sighed. "You're the one who's confused. You're looking for love. Am I right?"

He nodded. "That's right."

"Well?" She gave him a mystified look and patted her breasts.

"You're not what I had in mind."

"No?" she pouted. "Auntie's not good enough?" She leaned closer. "I suppose you've got your sights set on Papaya."

"Papaya?"

"You're like all the rest," Auntie lamented.

"I haven't met her."

"Did I give you my number?" She opened her worn purse, and a moth flew out.

"It's in a safe place," Wood assured her.

"This is hard on me." Her eyes were weary. "Not knowing, worrying about what's happening to you." She retrieved a pencil and notepad from her purse. "Beat your brains out with Papaya and the rest." She scrawled an address on the pad and tugged the scrap free. "Then you come get a night with Auntie."

She straightened herself, proud of her doggedness. "I'll be there." She grasped his hand, pressed the scrap of paper into his palm and folded his fingers around it.

An hour later Wood was back in his apartment, updating his log.

There was a knock on the door, and when he opened it, Mamey stood before him with a platter in her hand. "Look what arrived this afternoon."

Sections of papaya were arranged on the plate like the rays of the sun.

"*La fruta suprema*," Wood smiled, motioning her in.

They sat on the sofa together and sampled the sections.

"Exquisite, isn't she?" Mamey said.

"No other fruit compares," Wood agreed. "Is Papaya here on the Key?"

"Sometimes she is, and sometimes she isn't."

Wood took another section. "If I bumped into her on the street—"

"You'd know," Mamey nodded. "She makes a strong impression."

"You speak to her."

Mamey laughed. "Why would she have any interest in me? I hear about her at Buen Sabor. And at Sunday mass. She gives to our church."

"What does she look like?"

Mamey shook her head.

"Come on."

"I've never seen her, but— They say she's stunning. Gorgeous."

Wood could feel Mamey's unease.

"It's hard for a plain girl like me," she muttered.

"You're not plain."

"You say, 'Don't compare yourself to Papaya.' But there it is. She has the energy of five of us, and her spirits are always sky high."

"If you've never met her—"

"Everyone knows. She's vivacious and affectionate. But tasteful. Her warmth isn't cloying or vain. It's easy for her. Her reputation precedes her. Everyone expects she'll be flawless. They see perfection in whatever she does. You'd think she'd be exhausted by all the attention she gets.

"If that wasn't enough, her family is wealthy. I'm not alone. Every woman on the Key envies her. We all dream of being Papaya."

"She's unattached?"

"Don't get any ideas," Mamey said.

"A man can dream too."

"Have you ever seen a papaya tree?"

He shook his head.

"The trunk is straight and smooth, without branches. The fruit is on top, out of reach."

"What are you saying?"

"Papaya lives in a different world. The things I've heard—"

"Like what?"

"There are rumors about her sexual preferences. No man has been able to please her. Some women want to be like her, others want to be with her. But man or woman—no one measures up."

Wood picked up another section and turned it before him.

"Whatever it is that Papaya needs," Mamey said, "she hasn't found it."

5

It was scorching hot, so Wood put on his trunks and rode his bicycle to Taylor Beach.

The sky was blue, the sea pastel green, the sand white. There were people lying on towels and a couple walking the strand in the distance. He removed his shirt, descended the bank and threw himself into the water. A few minutes later, he was floating on his back, with his arms and legs limp and his eyes closed. A southern breeze rocked him.

The quiet was broken by the piping of terns. He parted his lids and saw the birds above him, swooping and diving. Thirty feet away, a woman was floating as he was, on her back. The wavelets were carrying him toward her.

Wood stared at the sky. A moment later, their bodies bumped.

The woman gave a startled cry and righted herself. He faced her as his feet touched the sand.

Her emerald eyes— There was so much raw feeling in them, Wood had a hard time speaking. "I'm sorry," would have been fine, or "Excuse me," or simply "Hello," but nothing emerged.

A small chin with a dimple dead center. Her lips, too ripe. Her hair too dark, too long— Her body seemed to tremble with the energy Wood saw in her eyes. Fine hands, fine fingers. A self-conscious smile. Her skin was reddish and smoky.

The water was at her bikini top. He was beside her, trying to hold up his end of the conversation.

The words were nothing. A hot day. The cool water. She lived in Old Town. The current pushed them, she raised her hand to his shoulder and the curve of her hip slid against his.

Then someone whistled. The woman turned toward the shore and peered at the trees. She was waving, pardoning herself, shouting to someone. Wood could see a man now, motioning to her. She gave Wood a helpless look, and then she was wading into the shallows.

Wood followed. Beyond the leaning trees, a car was waiting with its motor running. The woman reached the shore and stopped. She turned and looked back at him. Wood raised his arm, but it was too late. She slipped into the car, and it drove away.

He stood there, stunned. Then, as his clarity returned, he began replaying the conversation, trying to remember what she'd said. Was there some detail she'd shared, some clue that might lead him to her? She lived on the Key. Her eyes were emerald, her skin was bronzed, her bikini was blue— There was nothing else.

The worst luck. Women, so many, each with a different mind and heart. Now, just now, he'd bumped into the one he was meant to be with. But he had no idea who she was or how to reach her. Would he see her again—in Old Town, here on the beach? Tomorrow, next year, next week?

Then, all at once, it struck him.

Papaya, he thought.

"That's not Papaya," Mango said, shaking her head as she shook a drink.

The man beside Wood turned on his stool. "Don't be so sure," he disagreed. "She's dyed her hair." He was balding and his mouth sagged.

"You know Papaya?" Wood said.

"Sure."

"What does she look like?"

"She's a beauty." The man's lips spouted, as if he was whistling through the graveyard.

"The woman I met had darker skin," Wood said.

"She holds a tan. How tall was she?"

"Five-seven, five-eight. Her eyes were emerald green."

"Yeah. That's Papaya. You got a last look."

"Last look?"

"She's leaving the country."

"What? Is she coming back?"

The man shrugged and drank from his tumbler. "She's been here for over a year. She hasn't found what she wants."

"If she's leaving, good riddance." A younger fellow with beady eyes and a ponytail swung around.

"Papaya?" Wood was surprised.

The beady eyes fixed on him. "She killed my pal."

"Not really."

"Yeah, really. Henk was in such a fog, he stepped in front of a bus. He's not her only victim."

"Hell no," a third man joined in. "Fellow I worked with kept her pepped on coke. She drove him mad."

"And there's Willie," the beady eyes burned. "Poor kid gave up on women. He won't touch them now."

Mango set a blush down between Wood's hands. "They're pulling your chain."

"I need to find her."

"My shift just started," Mango told him. "Lime said she was here earlier."

Wood turned his head. Was he imagining it? Woven through the bar stench was a rarified fragrance. Intricate. Tropical. Seductive. "Where did she go?"

"Try Ten One Five," Mango suggested.

Wood put cash on the bar and flew through the door. He jogged up Duval, weaving through tourists. When he reached

Ten One Five, he scouted the tables outside and in. There were no single women.

"Has Papaya been here?" he asked the hostess.

"Who wants to know?"

"I'm a friend of hers," Wood said.

"Sure you are."

"Please. She told me to meet her here."

"Well—" The hostess wavered. "She had a reservation. She just cancelled."

"Do you know where she went?"

"Try Carrefour."

Wood continued up the street, passing strollers and early drinkers, trying to spot Papaya through the crowd. A shapely woman with dark hair had stopped to look through a store window. He came up behind her.

"Papaya?"

She turned. "I'm Cashew." She had pale skin, a hooked nose and dandruff.

When he reached Carrefour, Wood stopped a waiter on the patio. "I'm looking for Papaya."

"Haven't s-s-seen her," the waiter stammered.

"She was going to have dinner here."

The man seemed amused.

"She has dark hair," Wood said. "Five-seven and curvy."

"Pa-pa-paya is a redhead, and t-tall."

"She's a friend of yours?"

The waiter shook his head. "T-t-talk to C-c-cruiser Phil."

"Who's that?"

"He p-pilots a yacht." The waiter gave Wood the slip number.

The yacht was in the harbor, docked and vacant. Cruiser Phil was at the Bilge Pump, a bar across the way, holding forth to a crowd of tourists.

Wood edged through the gathering and slid onto a stool.

"Look all you like," Phil said. "Not a trace of her. As soon as you give up— There she is."

"Have you seen her recently?" a man asked.

"She just left," Phil said. "She was sitting right there." He pointed at Wood.

Wood stiffened and looked around. His seat was still warm.

Phil eyed him knowingly, sensing his frenzy. "Yup."

"Where did she go?" Wood demanded.

"Obsession." Phil swept his hand toward Wood, presenting him to the crowd like a sideshow freak. "No woman can touch Papaya," he chortled. "'Oh Lord— Just one more night.'" He snapped his suspenders.

Wood swore and stood.

The skipper stepped closer. "Look at this," Phil pulled up his sleeve. A tattoo of a halved papaya covered his bicep.

"Where is she?" Wood said.

"Talk to Coco."

"The old woman?"

Phil nodded. "She's close to Papaya."

"Who told you that?"

Phil made a simple face. “She’s Papaya’s aunt.”

“She’s everyone’s aunt,” Wood said.

He returned to Refugio, wrote out a message and gave it to Mango. “Do me a favor,” he said. “Pass this to Papaya the next time she’s in.”

“They’re a sorry lot—” Bijou was in the kitchen, stirring a salad. “The men who chase after Papaya.”

Wood frowned. “That’s unkind.”

“She’s great for business,” Tray said.

Bijou wiped her hands on a dishtowel. “You want a real woman, Wood.”

“Papaya’s real.”

Bijou looked at Tray, and the two of them laughed.

“That’s crazy,” Wood said. “Everyone on the Key knows who she is. You think she’s some kind of mass delusion?”

“Papaya’s perfect,” Tray said gently. “Every man’s dream. Perfect and unattainable.”

“She was as close to me as I am to you,” Wood insisted.

Bijou sighed.

Tray regarded her. “I think Wood should meet Nan.”

She looked doubtful. The two of them had obviously discussed this.

“Nan was here,” Tray said, “the night you met Tamarind.”

“The one who reads cards,” Wood nodded.

"Her given name's Banana," Tray said.

"She's bisexual," Bijou pointed out, as if that might dissuade him.

"Why Nan?" Wood asked Tray.

"She understands change," Tray replied. "She has a mutable soul."

After dinner, Wood returned texts from Callie and Piña. Then the two men retreated to the den upstairs.

"You're a bad influence," Tray said as they entered. "It's affecting Bijou, seeing how important love is to you. She's turning the heat up on me."

Wood regarded him. "She's committed."

Tray nodded. "I should be too."

"Aren't you?"

Tray sighed. "'It was a mistake to think I could see clearly into my own heart.' Proust again." He stepped toward the window. "The cemetery looks best when the sun's going down."

Wood followed, eyeing the gridwork of plots over Tray's shoulder. Oblique light gilded its vaults and monuments.

"A doctor named Von Cosel fell in love with a patient," Tray said. "She died and was buried there. One night, Von dug her up and took her corpse home with him. He has a fan club now."

Tray turned. "Bijou has enough conviction for both of us. She believes in goodness and right behavior. She thinks it's our mission in life to help each other."

"I love that about her," Wood said.

Tray seemed not to hear. "She doesn't know who I am."

Wood was silent.

"She thinks I'm so smart," Tray said. "I'm not that smart. She thinks I'm so helpful. I'm not that helpful. Most of my clients don't improve. Many get worse.

"I was with a gay couple this afternoon. The fighting was non-stop. The things they loved about each other have become things they hate. One is looking for a voodoo cure, the other just wants permission to leave. My practice is a daily reminder of how little I help."

"You're afraid of her faith in you," Wood said.

"I am. I'm afraid she'll wake up and see the truth."

The therapist seemed suddenly frail. "You understand yourself," Wood said.

Tray cocked his head. "Understanding doesn't make fears go away." He laughed. "They like being understood. It makes them feel important." He faced the armchairs.

The two men sat.

"When did the writing begin?" Tray asked. "Your passion for fiction."

"I was seven," Wood said. "A story was a private place, where I made the rules."

"In California."

Wood nodded. "McKittrick. A little oil town in the Central Valley. Hilly and dry. Pump jacks everywhere." In his mind, the iron horse heads were still dipping, feeding on the earth, sucking the black fluid from it. "My father left us. Mom was crushed. She remarried, then she got sick. She never recovered.

“My stepfather was a well puller,” he said. “I kept away from him, and he returned the favor.” The dusty shack was east of town, in a hollow surrounded by hills. A path wound through the pump jacks to the tar pools, and it was there he let his fantasies loose. “I’d pull some dead grass,” Wood said. “Make a seat for myself. The pools were magical. On a hot day, the surface would swell, like something was growing beneath. It swelled and swelled until a bubble blew up. You could watch it rolling there, oily and iridescent, purple and gold. I could see my reflection in it. I would talk to myself.

“When the sun went down, the bubbles collapsed. Skin hardened over them like a lizard’s back.”

Silence.

Then softly, Tray’s voice reached him.

“What you’ve told me about yourself and Vadette— You were desperate: two starving kids, trying to care for each other.”

“That’s what the Sacred Space was about, I suppose.” Wood faced him. “Her dad beat her. Her mom was an alcoholic.”

“The absent mother.” Tray closed his eyes. “She’s the cause of so many desperate desires. Longings that can’t be fulfilled.”

“Unborn twins,” Wood said.

Tray was nodding. “And Papaya.”

When Wood arrived at Nan's place, there was a note on the door: *Let yourself in.*

Another old Victorian, meticulously kept. The front room was filled with antiques. He sat on a velvet loveseat, admiring the woods and fabrics and the lamps with parchment shades. At the rear was a round table with three chairs, one with a high back.

Nan stepped from behind a drape. He smiled, and she tipped her head. She wore pants and a sport shirt, and had a no-nonsense air, but her fingers glittered with rings and an amulet hung from her neck.

She suggested Carol's Backyard for dinner. Wood phoned ahead, and they got a table. As luck would have it, Auntie Coco was there, and when he and Nan followed the hostess past the bar, Auntie turned and hooked her arm through his.

"You found me," she said.

Nan laughed and continued into the dining room with the hostess.

Auntie shook her finger. "You said you'd come visit."

"No I didn't."

The old woman was swaying. Wood grabbed her arm to keep her from falling. She was wearing a bracelet studded with jewels. As she steadied herself, she saw him eyeing it. "From an admirer," she winked.

"I met Papaya," Wood said.

Auntie looked surprised. "Did you?"

"A skipper—Cruiser Phil—said you were close to her."

"Papaya? Oh yes. We keep in touch. She's like you."

"Like me?"

The old woman beamed. "You're very special to Auntie." She cupped her left breast. "Whenever I see you, my milk comes down."

Wood stared at her, fished in his pocket and put a bill on the counter. "Have another on me." And he strode toward the table where Nan was seated.

They ordered and then, without any chitchat or preamble, Nan began to explain herself. She was headstrong, she said. Romantic, submissive with men—more than was healthy. Her comfort and self-control was with women.

"I'm still getting used to this," Wood confessed. "Things that would be unspoken anywhere else— Here, they're on the surface."

"People come to the Key to question themselves. To consider new possibilities." Nan leaned forward. "You were married."

Wood nodded. "The end was unexpected. By me. There's still pain."

"About women?"

"Yes." Wood met her gaze.

"You're alright, talking this way?"

"I want to be honest," he said. "I'm through lying to myself."

It started to rain as they were leaving Carol's. By the time they reached Nan's place, the sky was tumbling and the downpour was heavy. As she fumbled for her keys, Wood slid his arm around her waist.

She turned toward him.

"You're a seeker," he said.

"You're still healing."

"Help me, Nan."

She put her finger on his lips. Then she closed her eyes. Wood kissed her.

"Please," he whispered. What was it? Her directness, her intensity? "Nan, Nan—" It seemed that somehow his need had brought him to her.

"Our meeting isn't an accident," she said.

Wood kissed her again.

Her keys clinked on the steps, and the kiss drew out.

In her bedroom, Nan was self-assured, as if she had known him a long time. As if, in some prior life, it was she who had been his wife. She marshaled his movements with words. The promptings surprised him, as did the way she described what he was feeling.

The embrace grew heated. She softened, became more and more compliant, and as she grew softer, her guidance faded. With Callie's example in mind, Wood took the reins, whispering, seeking direction. When Nan answered, he followed carefully, asking again, giving as best he could. But with Nan it was different. Giving to her was easy because she was so conforming, so soft and close that his awareness of her as a foreign body dissolved.

He had never known sex could be so gentle. They were languorous and bemused, mashing a sweet pulp together, idling, dragging the moments out. As the sensations mounted, Nan preached patience, holding them off. The scents and tastes were delicate, so subtle they kept Wood mashing and guessing, trying to find the dominant note.

When the end approached, it came with a thrashing of leaves, the crunching of stalks and a rumble of thunder. It was outside them, beyond them, something over which they had no control. Afterward, he lay with his arms around her, listening to the rain pounding the roof.

"It's greater than us," he said.

"It's not even ours," she murmured.

Thunder punctuated her words. Lightning flashed in the windows.

She touched his temple. "What can I do?"

"Read the cards for me."

"Right now?"

Lightning struck nearby and the foundation trembled.

"Naked," Wood said. "In the dark."

Nan sat up. "I'll need a candle."

She took Wood's hand and rose with him, leading him into the front room. "You have a question to answer."

"Yes," Wood said as they approached the round table. "I

want to know if I'll ever find love. Real love. Love that will last."

Nan motioned him toward one of the smaller chairs. "Love means different things to different people." She struck a match and held it to the wick of a candle. "We will ask the cards to show us what love means to you."

Lightning flashed in the window behind her. Nan's silhouette appeared like a shadow in a mirror. She placed a deck of cards on the table and sat in the chair with the high back.

"We'll use a four-card spread, and you'll pick the Outcome." She passed her hand over the deck, fanning the cards across the table, facedown. "First, our Signifier."

Nan studied the backs of the cards, then selected one. She raised it, pondered it, then nodded and placed it on the table before him, faceup.

"This sets our direction."

"What is it?" Wood leaned closer.

"We've drawn The Tower," she said. "It signifies violent change."

Wood studied the image on the card.

"Tarot understands that trials are essential to life. The cards are designed to loosen our grip on the past and help us reach into the future. The Tower says that a change in your life will be sudden and violent. You might want things to return to the way they were, but change will occur regardless. Our objective for this reading will be to understand the journey you must make, and where it will lead you.

"Do you see yourself in the card?" she asked.

"The top of the Tower has been struck by lightning," Wood said. "The bolt has blasted its turret and thrown a man and woman down. They're falling to the earth."

Lightning cracked, shaking the building, silver light flashing in every window. Wood laughed.

Nan did too. "These things no longer surprise me." She put her finger on The Tower. "The protections of the past are gone. There is no shelter, no place of refuge. This card bespeaks illness, job loss, the breakup of couples or nations."

"I can't argue with that." He peered through the candlelight at Nan.

"It isn't all omen, Wood. Tarot teaches us to see beyond surface effects. The falling man— While the Tower was a stronghold built to protect him, it has become a place of isolation, a prison from which the lightning has freed him. He's falling, but he hasn't landed. His future is unknown. If he survives, he will no longer dwell in the clouds. He will be part of the world."

The candle flickered. Nan drew three more cards and set them facedown in a row below The Tower.

For years, Wood thought, his life had been governed by a sense of purpose, by decisions he made. Now, his fate was at the mercy of chance encounters, a message in a cookie, cards pulled from a deck.

"Tarot says this is of Most Influence in your life," Nan said, placing her finger on the card to the left. She turned it over.

"The Magus," she said.

"A magician?"

"Yes."

On the card was a picture of a strange creature, standing like a man, with a long head and ears like a donkey. He was naked and pink, with pink wings and a long pink tail coiled behind.

"His right arm is raised to the heavens," Nan said. "His left is aimed at the ground. He calls on higher powers to shape our destiny. But it's all hidden from view. He works from a secret place, acting invisibly, behind a veil."

"Nan—"

She paused. The thunder rumbled above them.

"I need some help with this."

"We're both in the dark right now," she said. "Give the cards time. They have more to tell us.

"Here we have Surface Reality," Nan put her finger on the card beside The Magus. She turned it over. "The Two of Pentacles. What do you see?"

"A man who's dancing, juggling two balls," Wood said. "A buffoon, someone without a care in the world."

"Like a boy playing with his toys," Nan said. "Or a man throwing himself at women, hoping things will turn out."

Wood stared at her.

"And here," Nan touched the card on the right, "is Deep Reality." She turned the card over. "The Five of Cups."

The image was grim. A man in a black cloak stood by a river, grieving. At his feet were empty cups.

"Abandonment and despair," Nan said. "A loss that's been

with you for a long time. Is there nothing beyond it? Will the cups ever be filled?"

"Where does the Magus come in?" Wood wondered.

"Behind the juggler's blind trust and the grieving man's loss," Nan said, "there is an invisible protector."

Wood frowned.

"Shall we look at the Outcome?" she said.

He nodded.

Nan gathered the remaining cards and fanned them. "Pick one."

Wood studied the array and extended his hand, pinching his fingers and pulling.

"You've taken two," Nan said.

"So I have."

She took the pair from him and set them beside The Tower, facedown. "Two Outcomes. Let's see what they are."

As she turned over the first, Nan raised her brows.

"The Seven of Cups." She sighed. "The card of self-delusion. The man has his back to us. He's fixed on the images hovering in the clouds before him. All he can see are his hopes and dreams."

Wood remembered the woman floating in the sea at Taylor Beach, and the things Tray and Bijou had said about Papaya.

"This man will never find love." Nan spoke softly. "He's wedded to his fantasies."

"There's another Outcome," Wood said.

Nan nodded, lifting the last card and turning it over.

Wood saw her smile.

"A happy ending," she said. "The Four of Wands. Harmony and home."

A man and a woman stood together, Wood saw. Their arms held blooms and were raised in celebration. Behind them was a village, and before them four poles supported a roof of green garlands.

"A grounded man," she said. "A romantic, but part of the world. He trusts his feelings and is guided by his heart. The love he's found is real and lasting."

She raised her head, straightened herself and looked around. "The storm is over, Wood." She eyed him with feeling. "You have a mate. She's waiting for you."

"You can see that?"

Nan nodded. "She sweeps the past away. She changes everything." Nan drew a breath, then reached to gather up the cards.

Wood set his hand on hers. "Is it you?"

She regarded him, then turned her head. "No. Not me."

"Are you sure?"

She rose and circled the table. As Wood stood, she embraced him and put her head on his shoulder.

"I'm too swayed by you," she said. "The Outcome I seek is the Ace of Wands. With the one I'm meant for, I won't lose myself."

In the flickering candlelight, Wood saw weariness in her eyes.

"And you—" She tried to smile. "You will struggle with

truth and illusion, wrestling with the servants of your invisible magus until you've found your due."

The sky was quiet now. No thunder, no rain, not even a drizzle.

"You're an unusual woman," he said.

"I have the power of projection."

Wood felt her hand touch his midriff.

"Shall I tell you a secret?" Nan said. "When you were inside me, I was imagining I was you. It was my strokes we were feeling."

The following day, Wood recorded the details of his time with Nan in his log. Despite the discouragement from Tray and Bijou, he was still thinking about the floating woman. Was Papaya the one who would change everything, or was she fantasy and self-delusion? Cruel circumstance had foiled their first encounter, but he told himself that she hadn't forgotten him. And he wouldn't forget her.

At noon, Wood put on shorts and his western vest and went walking. His feet took him south. He turned the corner and ducked beneath the Buen Sabor awning.

And there she was.

She recognized him instantly, and as he stepped toward her, she closed the distance, smiling, emerald eyes glittering, a bag of spiny green fruit in one arm. He hadn't exaggerated her warmth or her energy.

"I heard you were leaving the country," Wood said.

She looked surprised.

"Papaya?" he ventured.

"I'm flattered," she said. "But I'm not Papaya."

Was she being modest? he wondered. Or cagey?

"My name's Guanabana," she said. "Gwen for short."

"Are you—" Wood struggled for words. Her brows were black, as black as her pupils; her eyes were watching, and her brows were too.

"I live a few minutes from here," she said.

"Can I walk you home?"

Her apartment was five blocks east of his. As they approached her door, a neighbor waved and called out her name. Gwen waved back. Then, with what seemed an afterthought, she turned to Wood, smiling half to herself, and invited him in.

They stood in the kitchen and talked while she made drinks from the fruit she'd bought. Her hands opened and closed like elegant fans, and her fingers were delicate and exacting. With the moving blade and her glancing eyes, it was like watching a dancer.

When the drinks were ready, she led him outside. There was a swing lounge on the porch. They sat in it, and Gwen shared some of her history.

"I was born on the Keys," she said, "but I'm French in

a way. We ate French food and spoke French at home. My mother was a Cubano from Baracoa. My father was black, from Martinique."

"What brought you to Key West?"

"The beauty and the people. The freedom to be whoever you choose. And you?"

"Fate," he said. "I came here to meet you."

She nodded and sipped her drink, as if he'd remarked on the weather.

Wood talked about his separation and divorce. To his surprise, the information rolled off his tongue like ancient history. She seemed understanding. Nothing he said seemed to trouble her in the least.

"You're writing?"

"Developing material," he said, "for my next book."

"That sounds exciting." She checked the time. "I work at a seaplane charter near the airport. I have to be back by two."

"I want to see you again," Wood said. "Are you free tonight?"

Gwen clinked the ice in her glass. Then she smiled and nodded.

Walking back to his place, Wood felt an unusual ease. There had been no straining with Gwen, no gaps or stumbles. Words, looks and expressions, and a myriad feelings beneath—all had been woven together without a miscue. It was as if they had known each other in a previous life.

Gwen stepped onto the porch in a chartreuse dress, with pink lips and a white scarf around her shoulders. Wood hesitated, afraid to touch her, but she put her arm through his and they strolled down Catherine Street together.

"Our styles clash." She seemed amused. "I don't have any cowgirl clothes."

He was wearing a two-tone shirt with embroidered blooms on the yoke. "My fantasy of home."

"In California."

"I grew up near Bakersfield. You know where that is?"

She nodded. "They dress like that?"

"In the honky-tonks they do. They scrub off the grime and go dancing at night."

She wasn't in a hurry to eat. She suggested they follow Duval to the beach. Gwen had a lot to share—about her job, her sister and niece, the class she was taking at the Keys college. He said little, just taking it in. When they reached South Street, the crowds around the Southernmost Point appeared. Tourists were lined up to take pictures in front of a drum of painted concrete.

"Is it like that in the summer?" Wood said.

"Day and night, year round."

He laughed and shook his head.

"It makes them happy," Gwen said.

He peered at her. "You're forgiving." In the twilight, her hair looked darker. It fell in waves, over her shoulders and down her front. "I don't think I'm unreasonable or overly critical. But I've never been very forgiving."

"I'm too forgiving," she said. "It's one of my worst faults—believing what I want to believe instead of seeing what's there and accepting the truth."

He motioned and they crossed the roadway.

"I lie to myself," she said. She pushed her lips out, and they so dwarfed her small chin that she looked like a child.

"That's easy to do."

"I don't think I'm doing it, then suddenly I realize the lie is at the center of things. I'm building my life around it."

"You're talking about a man," he guessed.

She laughed. "What makes you say that?"

Gwen stepped ahead of him, leading the way past the cabana cafe, onto the beach. She stopped beneath a tall palm and took off her shoes. Wood did the same. Twenty feet away, a couple stood beneath another palm. They were holding each other and kissing.

Gwen seemed not to see the couple. Wood watched them, smiling. As Gwen turned to face him, he looked out to sea. The first stars were winking. A song started up, sounding from the cafe behind them.

Without a word, a woman sang, *without even one . . .*

Wood looked back. Gwen had inclined her head, listening. She glanced at him, then her gaze shifted, avoiding his.

She looked up at the fronds rustling above the kissing couple.

I knew it was you. I knew, I knew . . .

Wood laughed. Gwen faced him, but he was too self-conscious to meet her gaze, so he turned again to the stars and the sea. When he looked back, she had bowed her head. He waited a moment and she lifted her chin, but before their eyes met, her attention seemed drawn to something at the far end of the beach.

From that moment, the very first moment . . .

Gwen's lips parted. Her teeth glinted in the light from the cabana. "Let's walk by the water," Wood said, and he reached out his hand.

She took it without speaking.

As they descended the beach, the dry sand shifted beneath their feet.

"We're like this," Gwen said softly. "Don't you think? Like sand. You want to be whole, like a rock. You want to grab on to your life and move it from here to there. But it's all these tiny grains, moving in different directions." She regarded him.

"Maybe there's a secret. Something we don't understand." He thought of the Magus working behind a veil, acting invisibly.

"You have a need," Gwen said. "I can feel it."

"You can?"

She nodded. "You want to be loved."

"We all want—"

"Not like you."

"Is it that obvious?" he said.

She halted. "'Love me, please' is painted on your chest."

His heart sank. *I'm losing her*, he thought.

She raised his hand between them and put her other around it. "If we aren't looking for love," she said softly, "how will we find it?"

The sand was damp beneath them. The water was a few feet away. Pale wavelets lupped, while a hum and sough reached them from out at sea. Gwen let go of his hand.

"I hear a man's voice," she said, "when I'm falling asleep. Sometimes it sounds like my père. Sometimes it's the man I will marry. He can feel my need. If there's a secret, he knows it."

Wood was silent, surprised by her disclosure.

"I don't like thinking that I'm waiting for a man," she said. "That's so weak, so dependent. But the things I want most— I can't have them without him."

His lips were sealed, but his eyes searched hers.

"I don't talk this way with other people," she said.

"I like it. Don't stop."

Just ahead, the beach sand met a concrete pier, a flat gangway that led into the water. The waves splashed against it and the tide washed over it. Its end was lost in the gathering darkness. Wood started toward it. Gwen followed.

"Shall we?" he said.

She eyed the splashing waves. "We might be swept away."

"We might."

They reached the gangway, looked at each other and clambered onto it. The skim of water was thin near shore, but as they stepped out over the sea, it rose to their ankles. Waves struck the pier's sides, washing across it in angling sheets. An onlooker shouted. The kissing couple turned to watch.

Farther, the washing sheets threatened Wood's balance. He felt Gwen's hand tighten on his. The dimness swallowed their legs to the knees, the pier's edges came and went. How close were they to its invisible end? A few more steps, just a few more.

Wood planted his feet and faced her. Gwen raised her arms, resting them on his shoulders. He felt her fingers touching his neck, and he put his hands on her waist. It was narrow and firm. He bowed his head and their lips met as a wave hissed beneath them, slapping their knees. The kiss drew out. Wood's palm moved up her side, reaching her hair. He grasped a bundle of locks behind her head, feeling the silky strands slide through his fingers. He put his face to her neck and kissed it, getting her scent.

A crash and slapping, and they were hurrying back, slipping, struggling for balance. Wood reached the pier's footing and dropped over it, helping Gwen down. Her dress was splattered, his pants were wet to the thigh. They made their way back up the beach, and when they reached the palm, Wood lifted her in his arms and whirled her beneath it.

Gwen suggested they eat at the cabana. Wood insisted on taking her to Directement. But where they were didn't matter. They were speaking their hearts now, sharing their dreams.

"To know," Wood said. "Writing's just proof that I've made a discovery. It's wisdom I want."

"I want to be the beginning," Gwen said.

"Of what?"

"The source," she flared her eyes, "of harmony. Of joy. Of life."

When the meal was over, she mentioned there was a concert at Stages.

"Shall we go?" he said.

The crowd was a mix of bohemians, urbanites and tourists—a mingling only the Key could arrange. The music was loud, wordless and dreamy. A man played a giant sax, while a woman hit chords on a guitar drowned in chorusing. Conversation was difficult, and the flow of thoughts and feelings between them ceased. Gwen was a stranger again.

The music was like a soundtrack for the Sacred Space, a refrain for lost souls submerged and rolling in an inky pool. Wood fought the association, but the sounds took him back to Vadette. He found himself adrift in memories, drunk with regret, plagued by all the things he might have done before she left.

He offered to walk Gwen home before the concert ended.

"Are you alright?" she asked.

The streetlamps were lit, and the night was quiet.

"I was thinking about *Unborn Twins*," he said.

"I snuck a look at it this afternoon."

Wood could hear her unease.

"Was it really like that?" Gwen asked.

He shook his head.

"Is that what you want with a woman?"

"No."

"Is it too soon?" she said.

He could see the doubt in her eyes.

"I hope not." Wood clasped her hand.

When they reached her place, she invited him in.

He sat at the kitchen table. She brewed some tea, poured him a cup and set it before him. Then she kissed him. A long kiss, with a world of feeling inside it. Wood's confidence returned, and along with it, his desire.

He rose.

Another kiss, this one set in motion by him. He touched her scarf and began to untie it. "I can't say no," she whispered.

Wood led her down the hall, toward the bedroom. In the doorway, a kiss much gentler than those before. Then they crossed the threshold.

Gwen unbuttoned his shirt. He unzipped her dress.

She moved to the bed and turned back the covers. He came up behind her, circling her with his arms. Her flesh felt soft. Her skin was warm, so thin that he worried his fingers might tear it.

He lifted her onto the bed.

Guanabana, he thought, wondering what pleasures the fruit would reveal. But Gwen was unlike the others. She acted as if she was more than a gift, as if he was more than a giving recipient. She acted as if he was somehow deserving. In some forgotten time, he'd been part of her life, part of her growth.

A strange idea—that he had fed her, nurtured her, watched and waited; and now, after so much labor and love, the time had arrived.

Together they peeled the skin, parted the membranes, made careful slices. A wealth of fragrant pulp was inside, flowing with juice. The taste was subtle; sweet, sharp and acidic, but fresh and pure. This rare bounty, this fruit they had grown together in a previous life, was a long drink of water from a crystal stream. You'd want it with you under any condition.

There was no hesitation now, no holding back. The savor was on his tongue, and the acquaintance grew quickly. The fruit's deep character revealed itself, along with whiffs of its history. Beneath the tropical tartness was the taste of shadowy places. Places where the trees that bore this fruit had first rooted, where the spirits of lovers still came and went.

The place was a darkened garden, and the boughs were bare. Between the trees, Wood could see ghostly bodies shifting—standing, kneeling, lying together on the fertile earth. He and Gwen were among them, breathless, whispering, limbs entwined. The garden was on an island. Their bed was the soft loam, and the night breeze warmed them with a sheltering sigh.

They were silhouettes, just silhouettes, merging and parting in the spectral light. Had they once been one? If they had, it was long ago; too far in the past to remember. Had they ever known sun? How long had they wandered the island?

How many times had they lain in this garden, still fruitless and barren?

The breathing and clasping mounted, the writhing and whispers—

The ghostly embrace was reaching its conclusion. A quaking shook the garden, taking hold of them both. As the jolts grew fiercer, Wood felt Gwen's heart touching his own. And with the contact came a gripping and wrenching. Grief, buried deep inside him, grabbed on—even as his body fought to expel it.

Grief that the garden of love had been a dream for so long. And fear—that the pleasure he felt was fleeting, only illusion. The Seven of Cups. There were other islands and other gardens, and lovers who had made their Eden a home. But here, the branches were bare and the lovers were ghosts.

The quaking shook him, every nerve enjoined, every muscle jerking; and as the powerless moment arrived, it dashed his thoughts. His mind was, all at once, an open vessel, and his ghostly partner was with him—foreign, shattered as he was, helpless, quaking— As shocked by his presence as he was by hers.

The air was moist and the boughs were dripping. The trees were crying, and so was she. Gwen was there with him, her lips to his ear, her hand on his thigh. Somehow she understood.

Wood's grief let go. Grief for the sham of love with Vadette. Grief for the suffering parent, grief for the forlorn child— It was safe to grieve, because the fear wasn't real—the fear that he would never find love again.

Gwen's cheek touched his and their tears flowed freely, streaming together.

They spent the next morning in bed. Their bodies talked, then they gave their bodies a rest and used their heads. They shared trifles, memories, amusements. On occasions, a French word would slip from Gwen's lips—an endearment or an exclamation. When she was thoughtful, the tail of her right brow arched. At times, her face was dyadic: her left eye relaxed, interior and thoughtful, wistful or sad; the right eye piercing, alert, surprised, curious or suspecting.

"Describe the perfect man," Wood said.

"I know him completely, to the bottom of my being. And he knows me, in the same way. Why are you smiling?"

"Because you're serious." He spoke gently, with fondness.

At midday, they rode their bikes together. Gwen's came from the same shop, and she knew Sapodilla. Gwen laughed and beamed as she pedaled, her long hair swept back, undulating on the breeze. They ended up at Taylor Beach. On impulse, they reenacted the bump that brought them together, then they sat on the sand and stared at the clouds. Gwen liked Las Nubes, so they went there for dinner. They were back in her apartment by nine, undressed and entwined.

The acute sensations, the depth of feeling— Wood held his breath, and the two went deeper. Headlong and heedless, they were diving together. His tact, his control, his forbearing was stripped away.

"Mon cher," Gwen whispered.

The ceiling dissolved, exposing a night full of stars. Then the stars detached and were showering down.

"Mon cher, mon cher, dévore-moi."

Wood felt her heart again, and the ghost emerged from hiding—the ghost of himself, the stranded soul in the garden, the silhouette lurking between the trees.

He was in the garden, but the night had ended. The sun was rising, and it lit a strange scene. The garden was on the brow of the island, with a view of the sea. As the morning rays reached him, his body grew solid and his skin turned pink.

He wasn't a wandering spirit. He was a boy. The crowns of the trees crowded the sky, and wherever he looked, he saw fruit—hanging from branches, ready to pick. On the ground before him was a giant guanabana, sliced and open, ready to eat.

Around it were things a boy likes. Jacks and firecrackers, a slingshot and flagstaff, and a folding knife. Amid a scatter of candy and coins was a purple top. He knelt and grasped it, touching its tip with his thumb.

He was here to play. Paper airplanes caught his eye, riding the breeze. High above, a kite was sailing. Wood picked up a whistle and blew it. All he had known of boyhood was want and need, and the wish to escape. Here, with a bounty of Gwen and toys aplenty, he could enjoy a youth that he'd never had.

Was this love's secret? Was it really that simple?

6

Alone in his apartment again, Wood returned to his log. It was hard to put what he'd experienced in words. His time with Gwen seemed like a dream, something he'd imagined.

His pen ran dry before noon, so he walked to the drugstore. As he was leaving, he ran into Piña. He wanted to share the news about Gwen, but it seemed too fresh, too private. On the way back, he got a call from Callie. He dodged her questions, and they talked about her play. Then he texted Mamey, and Tray and Bijou, but he kept Gwen a secret from them too. He wasn't sure why.

They spoke during her break. Gwen had a test coming up and she needed her free time to study. They agreed to meet for lunch in a couple of days.

When darkness fell, Wood headed for Hao Zhidao. Along

Duval, barricades were being unloaded from trucks. "What's going on?" he asked a man walking beside him.

"Fantasy Fest," the man replied.

Down the street, Wood noticed posters on walls and in shop windows, along with placards that advertised costumes and body painting.

The evening special was Pickled Pork with Bitter Melon. He hurried through the meal, eager to see what the cookie would say. Guava stood close while he broke it open.

A CHANCE MEETING CHANGES EVERYTHING, the fortune read.

Wood looked up. "They're slipping. The meeting's behind me."

"There's a festival party tomorrow night," Guava said.

"Fantasy Fest."

She nodded. "I want you to be my escort."

"I've met someone."

"'Escort' I said. I'll pick you up at eight. Give me your number." Guava took the fortune, and as Wood spoke, she recorded his phone number on the slip of paper. "There will be people in costume."

"Do I need one?"

"Your cowboy clothes will be fine."

The party was at a physician's house, modern but built in the island style, with an electric ceiling that slid back to reveal the sky. Scores of silver helium balloons were secured by black ribbons. Tugging on one, Wood was surprised by the strength of the gas. When the ribbon came loose, the balloon rose through the gap in the ceiling, into a night sequined with stars.

While Guava helped the physician's wife with hors d'oeuvres, Wood mingled. A woman named Fig struck up a conversation with him. She wasn't in costume, but she was gritty and droll, and he enjoyed her wit. Fig explained that the festival was a tribute to the bounty of fruit.

Unexpectedly, a third guest joined them—a masked woman. She was tall, a platinum blonde with a wide forehead and hair parted far to one side. A white comber rose over her black velvet mask, waves falling to her shoulders like frozen water. The blonde didn't speak. She stood six feet from Wood and danced by herself. Her dress had a plunging neckline, a deep vee that reached her navel. On her arms and sides, the fabric's rosy gold framed her body. The flesh in the vee was painted with black seeds. She looked like a giant papaya with a section carved out of her center.

"Look who's here," Fig said, rolling her eyes.

Wood laughed.

The masked woman acted like she hadn't noticed either of them. Wood tried to acknowledge her, then he tried to ignore her. She had prominent breasts with unnatural points. Her dress barely hid her nipples. Fig was irritated. "Excuse me," she said, glaring at the woman.

The blonde moved closer, and her movements grew more exaggerated. Then all at once, she halted. Her arms fell to her sides and she met Wood's gaze, hair white as ice, eyes icy blue. Fig made a sound of contempt, turned on her heel and left. Wood started to introduce himself, but the blonde walked right past him.

For laughs or curiosity— Wood followed her.

She crossed the room and halted before a picture window. Wood's steps slowed. He was thinking of Gwen, feeling guilty. The woman was regarding her reflection, smoothing the fabric over her hip. Through the window, on either side, the lights on Duval glittered through the fog.

"A striking view," Wood said.

The blonde looked over her shoulder.

"I'm new on the Key," he said.

"And wretched," she nodded. "Don't think I can't see."

"Keep it between us, will you?"

"The little lost lamb." She turned, reached out and mussed his hair.

"What are you doing?"

"Messing with you," she said. "I like that getup. And those boots."

Wood was wearing double-pleated pistol pants and a gaucho shirt.

Two men passed, greeting the woman jokingly. "There

you are," one said. "So glad you could make it," the other chimed in. She ignored them.

Wood scanned the crowd. "There's another papaya by the punchbowl."

"She's a fake."

He laughed and shook his head. "If you knew—"

"Oh I know," the woman said. "You've been looking for me."

Wood stared at her.

"I heard from Stammering Stan," she said. "You left a note at Refugio."

He was speechless.

"Well," the woman turned her palms up. "Out with it."

Wood peered into her eyes. There was naked contact.

A dwarf in a double-breasted suit stepped between them. He had a trimmed goatee and a drink in each hand. He raised one to the woman who called herself Papaya. "I'm her date," he told Wood. "Move along."

Papaya untied a helium balloon and looped the ribbon through a buttonhole in the dwarf's coat. She fastened a pair around his wrists and shoulders. As Wood watched, the dwarf rose into the air. He floated above the heads of the partygoers; then, kicking his legs and waving his hands, he was carried through the gap in the ceiling.

"Let's dance." She grabbed Wood's arm.

A slow song was playing. The woman led him to the center of the room, circled him with her arms and began to dance. A space cleared around them. Her moves became brazen. Her hands wandered his back, her middle writhed and she flung back her head. Wood was onstage, and the crowd was a circle of eyes.

"What is this?" he said.

She smiled as if there were things about him only she knew. But what could that be, aside from his interest in meeting Papaya? Her overtures were phony, he thought. For show.

When the music ended, the woman offered her lips for a public kiss. Wood laughed and turned away.

She grabbed his hand and pulled him into a dark corner.

"You're frightened," she said.

"Can I see your face?"

The woman put her back to the party, and raised her mask. Her brow was high and wide. The bridge of her nose was perfectly straight, and her lips were too, straight and silvery. A beautiful woman, Wood thought.

"Get me a blush," she said, replacing her mask.

Wood returned with goblets, and they talked while they drank. She remained in character, stewing about Papaya's endless search for a mate. She seemed deadly serious, and her eyes never stopped moving. When she laughed, Wood heard something darker—gloom or despair.

Guava interrupted to say she was feeling sick and was heading home. Wood offered to go with her, but she said she'd be fine on her own. When he turned back, the woman dressed like Papaya was gone.

He wandered from room to room with the blush in his

hand, indifferent, not seeking her out. But curious nonetheless. She was on the balcony, talking to a group of men. He moved to within a dozen feet of her, then swung half around and began speaking to the woman beside him. When he looked again, he had Papaya's attention. She tipped her head up, as if to motion him closer. Through the holes in her mask, her eyes were piercing. But when he started toward her, she turned away.

Wood cursed her and laughed at himself. He got another drink, and then scouted the front room again. She was nowhere in sight. He ambled down a hall, peering through doorways. She was in the library, with a half-dozen guests around her. As he watched, she removed a man's cravat and bandaged his arm with it. She took the scarf from a woman's shoulders and tied it around her waist. Wood strode up to the group, moving behind her, his eyes on her back. The group grew silent.

"Papaya," he said in a commanding voice.

His hand rose toward her neck, then stopped in midair.

"What do you want?" she said without turning.

The stares burned him. He imagined they were melting his face. His flesh was dripping like wax on his chest.

Wood hurried out of the room.

He found himself in the foyer, hunched by the coat closet, sweating and trembling. Finally his pulse eased and slowed.

Outside, he hurried along the dark street, swearing, angry he'd let himself be sucked in. A convincing performance. Alluring, frustrating, impossible to please. A woman who could make a man step in front of a bus. As soon as Wood saw a pink cab, he hailed it, shouting. Then he was speeding away, putting distance between himself and the strange woman.

The next morning, Wood called Tray.

"That's crazy," Tray said.

"Twisted. Perverse."

"Just what you need."

"Whoever she is," Wood said, "I'll probably never see her again. You're going to the Fest?"

"We stay away," Tray replied. "It's tens of thousands of people, from everywhere. They come here to do things they wouldn't do at home. You'll enjoy it."

Wood recorded what happened at the party in his logbook. Then he dressed and called Gwen. She thought she'd done well on her test. She would meet him for lunch as they'd planned. He arrived at her apartment a half-hour early and waited on the porch.

She pulled up in her car, parked on the street and stepped toward him, beaming and swinging her purse. Her eyes were so bright, her smile so wide— The sight was a shock. She was so open, so intensely alive.

I'm really in love, Wood thought.

No woman on earth could compare with Gwen.

They kissed on the porch, and then she opened the door, and they were stumbling inside, stripping off their clothes. The look in her eyes— They were bottomless wells, unwavering, ancient. What he saw wasn't just love, it was something timeless. The look of forever.

On the bed, they found a new kind of frenzy. Gwen was wild, fierce and aggressive. She shrieked and straddled him, grabbing, eyes gleaming. And that provoked the wildness in him. It was like an account he'd read of a deadlock between a squid and a whale. How many limbs did she have? They were all wrapped around him. His jaws clenched and he plunged, taking her with him.

The sea churned, the squid shook, the whale's throat thundered. The embrace was a death grip, and as the violence mounted, the coast nearby was sucked into its vortex. An island planted with gardens and orchards—they were dragging it with them. No power on earth could tear them apart. The squid tightened her limbs and the whale dove for the bottom.

They found their moment down there, and once they were spent, they remained there together, with the drowned groves and sunk plantations, on the sea floor. The currents grew tranquil, the ocean grew calm.

Gwen had left a window open. Outside, the sun shone through a crown of fluttering leaves. Coins of light passed between the parted curtains, gilding their bodies and dappling the sheets. At the foot of the bed, as Wood watched, the island they'd dragged to the bottom surfaced like a buoyant Atlantis, shedding streams of sea.

The haven that met his eyes still had its orchards and its bounties of fruit. But the garden on the shore before him was changed. Love had transformed it. A single picking—a great guanabana—stood on the sand, open and waiting. The boy's playthings were gone, except for one: a slingshot made from a forking branch. The boy had plucked out the look of forever and put it in the slingshot's crotch. The ancient eye was his now, to keep or send flying.

Gwen sat up.

"What's your next book about?" she asked.

Wood regarded her. "I'm not sure."

"You're always writing."

He shook his head. "Just notes about what's happening to me." The disclosure was painful. "*Unborn Twins* depended on Vadette. When the marriage ended—"

"I want to know about her."

Wood sighed.

"Please," she said.

So, cautiously, he explained how he and Vadette had met. Then, in response to Gwen's questions, he told her how they got married and how good he imagined the marriage was. He described how he'd been stung, and how he discovered Vadette was lost to him.

Gwen had trouble understanding. "What was wrong? Why did she give you up?"

Wood spread his hands. "Who is she really? If I knew, I'd tell you. I was in love with my dream of her. I can only tell you about that."

"The Sacred Space."

He nodded. "I wish I had kept the dream to myself. It's out there now. There's no taking it back."

"You're ashamed of your book."

"I guess 'shame' is the word. I don't know where I go from here," he confessed. "*Unborn Twins* found an audience. People who want to believe that love is like that. I'm not going to spin more lies. For me or for them."

"You can't stop writing." Gwen spoke uncertainly. "How will you live?"

"It's what I've always wanted to do," he said. "But right now, nothing makes sense. Nothing but you."

Silence. Gwen reached for his hand.

She asked about his childhood, so he told her about McKittrick and the dusty shack, and his mother, and the stories he made up by the tar pools.

"How old were you when she died?" Gwen asked.

"Nine."

"Tell me about her."

Wood drew a breath. "She got sick when I was three. She told me that. It's not something I remember. She had trouble walking. One day she gave up. Her legs were too weak. She sat in a chair at first. For a while, she cooked. Then she couldn't. There was nothing I could do to help her."

"What about your stepfather?" Gwen asked.

"He acted like it wasn't happening. Once she was confined to her bed, she began to waste away. She got thinner and thinner. At the end, I was afraid to touch her. She was so feeble, so frail."

"She wished she could still be a mother to you," Gwen guessed.

"Maybe," he said. "She lived in a silent world. I would speak and she wouldn't answer. I didn't know what she was thinking or feeling. I wasn't sure she knew I was there." His hand lay open on his thigh, as if a bird had flown.

"After she died, the shack was a gloomy place. My stepfather— He kept us going, but we barely spoke. When I wasn't in school, I was at the pools. Friends met me there. In the spring and fall, the tar was goopy, like black clay. You could make things out of it. In the summer, it was liquid, and with matches, you could light the gas bubbles. They'd burn like candles on a birthday cake.

"We'd throw things in—things we'd taken from home—and watch them sink. The fumes made you dizzy. We would threaten to push each other in."

Gwen shuddered. "When we lived on Key Largo, the kids played 'Quicksand' in the swamp. Weren't you worried?"

"Oh yeah. If the tar was thick, you'd sink slowly. If it was hotter, you'd go down fast. Your friends would be afraid to tell anyone. You'd just disappear. No one would ever see you again." Wood laughed. "I realized later— That's where the Sacred Space came from. The warm, dark place; the secret place with a secret companion. My twins were born in a pool of tar."

After work, Gwen met him at his apartment. On the way to dinner, they saw the first event of Fantasy Fest, a block fair on a street west of Duval. Latin music reached them, along with the smell of roasted plantains. The street was jammed with people and vendors. A black man stirred a vat of curry with a giant spoon. A fat lady used tongs to turn skewers on a grill.

"It goes till midnight," Gwen said.

No one on the street was in costume.

"It's tame today," she said. "By the weekend, most of them will be naked."

He faced her. Was she serious?

"They paint their bodies," Gwen said. "There's a parade down Duval."

"Something you do?"

She shook her head. "The Fest isn't for me."

He had a table reserved at Carol's Backyard, on the deck overlooking the sea. "You're treating me like Papaya," Gwen laughed as they crossed the deck. She was modest in public. When a couple of men stared, she averted her gaze.

After they ordered, the talk grew serious. The subject was history again, but this time the questions were his. He started by asking about her father.

"The second heart attack killed him," Gwen said.

"The jobs, the physical labor?"

"The jobs and the stress," she said. "He was determined to send me to college. He worked fourteen hours a day. Weekends too. I was a terrible burden. When I fell in love— I thought I was smarter, I thought I knew better. I was sixteen.

"Josu was a year older. Tall, fine looking. Headstrong and black, like my père."

"You got married," Wood said, "at sixteen?"

"In Cuba," she nodded. "Nobody knew. I was already pregnant. I lost everything, Wood. My père, my baby— Josu didn't want her. I'll never outlive that. It was unforgivable."

"You let him convince you."

"I can't blame him," she said. "I should have protected my baby."

"But you left him. You went to college. Your père would be proud."

"It took me two years," she said. "He was out every night with other women. I pretended it wasn't happening. I couldn't let go." She looked around them, as if she feared people at other tables were listening. "I wanted to believe he was like my father."

Wood moved a stray lock that had fallen across her eye.

"Raina, my older sister," Gwen went on, "she thought I'd live through it, and that gave me hope. But it took a long time. Josu left so many scars. I served his needs without getting anything. I thought I was frigid. In college, I met an older man. He was loyal and kind. He worshipped me. I used him—unfairly—to find myself. I didn't love him. I brought him so much pain. I'm ashamed of that too."

Dusk had come. On the rail of the deck, three candles were burning. Had Gwen ignited them with a glance?

"Does this change things?" she asked.

Wood shook his head. "Our failures, our sadness— They speak to each other. I feel closer to you."

They returned to her apartment for the night.

In the late hours, when their passions were exhausted, they lay facing each other. Gwen wore only her earrings. She was never without them, Wood had learned, even when she slept. He stroked her cheek with his finger. She put her hand behind her neck, bracing her head, staring at him, lips parted as if she was seeing something for the first time. A smile reshaped her lips. Her eyes creased and softened.

"With you," she said, "it will all work out."

The next morning, through the dimness, Wood saw her tiptoe across the floor. Was she afraid she would wake him? Did she want him to see her lightness? Or was it just her idea of how a woman should touch the world?

He stood behind her, watching her brush her hair.

The darkest chocolate, impossibly fine, with the subtlest undulations. As the bristles ran through it, the light infused its strands, pulling them straight, then relaxing them back. Her fingers followed, slender, sensitive, sliding between.

"Do you like my hair?" She looked back.

"There's music in it."

"It's soft," she said, moving the brush again.

"And flowing. The long lines of a violin."

Back at his place, Wood recorded Gwen's story in his log. In the middle of his entries, he got a call from Guava. The woman he'd met at the party had asked the host to pass a message to him. Would he call? Guava gave him the number.

Wood completed his log entry, glancing now and again at the number. When he was finished, he walked to South Beach, where he wound his way through the palms and lounge chairs and white umbrellas. A breeze made the umbrellas pulse like jellyfish, while the palm fronds above swept the air like combs.

Gwen's anguish for her lost child brought Callie's misfortune to mind. He had to talk to her. On his way back from the beach, he called. She didn't pick up, and he was nervous about leaving a message, so he called again when he reached his apartment. Still no answer. He called a third time and a fourth. On the last, she picked up and began to spout.

"Wood?" she said. "Wood who? Where the hell have you been? I miss you."

"I miss you too. Can I see you this afternoon?"

Callie was suspicious. "Something's wrong."

"Or tonight, after the show."

"What is it? Tell me now."

"I'd rather—"

"Now," she demanded.

"I've got bad news. I've met another woman."

"What?"

"I'm in love with her, Callie. I know you'll understand."

"You're wrong. I don't understand," she fumed. "Who is this woman? I played a tragedy for you. My tragedy. I never do that!"

"I adore you. I want to see you, if you're okay—"

"I'm not okay," she sobbed. "You're bringing the curtain down."

Then the line went dead.

Wood turned, gazing at the walls and through the window, shaken, regretful. He hadn't meant to hurt her, but what had happened was cruel. His eye fell on the phone in his hand. He saw the message from Guava, with Papaya's number. Without knowing why, he rang it. No one answered. "It's Wood," he said dully. Then he disconnected and turned his phone off.

Hoping to clear his head, he descended the stairs and headed for Duval. The sidewalks were mobbed with festival visitors. A couple and their kids were posing for a photo with three drag queens outside the club where they worked. A drunk wove through the crowd on his bicycle, turned the corner, ran into a newspaper stand, struck his head and fell off his bike. Iguana Bob stood beside Piña's tattoo parlor with his pets wrapped around his neck. Wood stepped inside.

The parlor was packed. In the front, a half-dozen artists were talking with women, sketching and gesturing. At the rear, the tattoo machines were buzzing. As Wood made his way through the crowd, he spotted Piña, stooped over a flabby man lying facedown. She wore rubber gloves and had a headlamp mounted on her brow. Piña stretched the man's skin with her left hand and held the buzzing machine in her right. It had a pink barrel and a chrome tip.

"Woody—" She beamed.

Her machine was like a vibrating ice pick. He could see the needle piercing the flesh. A giant halved papaya was taking shape on the man's back.

"Nice work," Wood said. "*La fruta suprema.*"

"Everyone wants Papaya."

"You know her?" Wood asked.

Piña laughed. "She's a fairy tale some boys made up."

"Hey." The man on the table raised his shoulders.

"Relax." Piña pushed him back down.

Wood leaned closer. "Can we talk in private?"

"It's awfully busy." She switched her machine off. "Make it quick." She motioned him toward the supply alcove.

Wood took a breath. "I've fallen in love with someone," he said. "I care about you. I don't want our friendship to end."

"That's why you came by?"

He nodded. "Tell me it's okay."

Piña frowned. "It's okay, I guess."

"How are things with Stubby?"

Piña huffed and shook her head.

"Papaya's feeling neglected," the flabby man shouted.

Wood squeezed Piña's arm. Then he made his way through the crowd and out of the shop.

He met Gwen at Smathers Beach on her lunch break. He brought Cumin Shrimp and Beef with Cabbage. It was blowing, but they sat on the sand in the lee of a dune and ate from the cartons with chopsticks.

"Can I ask you a sensitive question?" Gwen nodded to herself.

"Fire away."

"You were seeing other women before we met."

"Why do you ask?" Wood said.

"This morning, one of our pilots invited me out. I said no. I don't want to see anyone but you."

Wood met her gaze. "I feel the same way. I'm not looking for love from anyone else."

Gwen drew a shrimp from the carton with her chopsticks and held it toward him. Wood opened his mouth, and she set it on his tongue.

"I like restaurants," she said.

He could see the qualification in her eyes. "But?"

She smiled. "I want to cook for you tonight."

He swiped his head, like a horse pulling at its reins. "Cozy." The irony in his voice surprised them both.

Gwen recoiled as if she'd been bitten. She turned and stared at the water.

Where did that come from? he thought. *You've hurt her.*

Wood's stomach was churning. He was upset about something—Callie's anger, or the call from Papaya or whoever she was. Why had he returned it?

"I'm sorry," he thought. *"Yes, please. I love the idea."* That's what Gwen needed to hear. But the words didn't come, and the silence drew out.

Finally he reached for the bag.

"Fortune?" he said, passing it to her.

Gwen exhaled, fighting herself. She tried to smile and fished in the bag.

There was only one cookie. She handed it to him. Her brows were peaked, and her lips were sealed. Her green eyes had a crushed look. They had never been emeralds. They were soft as gelatin. What had he done?

Wood turned the cookie between his fingers, then he cracked it open. YOU WILL BE TEMPTED, the fortune said.

"May I?" Gwen held out her hand.

But as he was passing it to her, a gust circled the dune and took it from between his fingers, and the ill-boding prophecy blew out to sea.

That night he took Gwen to Ten One Five. She had returned from work with her spirit back, but as the meal wore on, she seemed to lose it. She pecked at her food, and when she spoke, it was in clipped phrases.

"You're brewing about something," Wood said.

She nodded. Gwen looked at her plate. "I don't want to pry."

"That's alright."

"You said you had to take out a loan to get through college. Have you paid it back?"

Wood shook his head.

"Your apartment, this dinner— Where does the money come from?"

"My publisher," he said.

"There's a lot left?"

He took a breath. "Not a lot."

"Eating in a place like this doesn't matter to me. I want you to know that. I can be frugal. I've lived that way all my life. There are other things—" She stopped herself.

"Other things?"

"Things that cost money," she said. "Things that are more important."

"Such as?"

She sighed. "I'm sorry, Wood. I really am. I can't help myself. I can't stop thinking about it."

"About what?"

"Having children. With you."

Wood was stunned.

"So little time has passed," she said, faulting herself. "We're still learning about each other. But— I feel so close to you." She sounded helpless.

"I'm sorry for the 'cozy' remark. It was callous. Cruel."

"It hurt me," she said. "But it got me thinking. Could you be a father? Do you want a family? Is that something you've ever considered?"

Wood tipped his head back, as if what she'd said was a lot to swallow. "Sure. Someday." His smile was matter-of-fact, but his eyes darted.

When dinner ended, they walked to Truman Annex and wandered the lawns and walkways beneath the park lights. Wood remembered the couple in the Four of Wands and the arbor roofed with garlands. They reached the waterfront, and as they approached the prow of the Coast Guard cutter moored there, Gwen stopped and faced him. Her lips pouted, dwarfing her small chin. Then she stood on her toes and put her lips to his.

When the kiss ended, Wood drew back. Her collar was crooked.

"I worry too much," Gwen said. "It's not as bad, when I'm with you."

"I should worry more. Keeping a diary isn't writing. I need to get back to work." He straightened her collar.

"I believe in you," Gwen said.

There was passion in her voice, but her belief seemed groundless. She had no idea how rudderless he was. If she'd asked him what he intended to "get back to work" on, he wouldn't have had an answer. He had no concept, no story, no plan.

Gwen knew her own heart, and she said things that were brilliant sometimes. But she wasn't as smart as Vadette. Or as strong, or as independent. And when she lost her bearings, the distractions showed. As they were leaving the restaurant, she'd put her lipstick on wrong. He used his thumb now to remove the deviating red.

"I love your humanity," he said.

"My imperfections, you mean?"

He shook his head. "You're an honest woman, not a puzzle or a maze. The more time we spend with each other, the more I know who you are. You're not afraid to be weak, not afraid to feel shame, not afraid to admit that you're hurt and to show it."

Her eyes shone. "What a wonderful thing to say."

"Is there a danger—" He squinted.

"Of what?"

"So much of love is mystery," he said. "Mystery and magic. What if it's lost? What happens if it vanishes?"

They were eye to eye, but Gwen was silent.

"Love helps people build a life together," she said finally. "They need each other to do that. I'm in love with a man named Wood, and I want to build a life with him."

"That's a little frightening."

"It frightens me too," Gwen said.

They spent the night at her place, and the next morning they stopped at Buen Sabor and bought fruit pastelitos. Mamey was on duty, and to avoid any impropriety, she pretended Wood was a stranger. But when he paid for the pastelitos, he introduced her to Gwen as "a close friend." Then he turned to Gwen and kissed her. "I found her," he told Mamey.

Gwen went to work, and Wood returned to his apartment. He called Tray and Bijou and told them about Gwen. They congratulated him. Then he called Nan. She didn't answer, so he left her a message. The man falling from the Tower had landed, he said. He'd found the woman who was going to change everything. At the end of the day, Mamey knocked on his door. She had a hundred questions. They sat on the sofa, and Wood gave her the details.

When he lay down that night, he neglected to turn off his phone's alert. At 2 a.m., it woke him. He silenced the phone but had trouble returning to sleep. He sat up in bed and checked for messages. There was a text from the woman who called herself Papaya. "Plagued by you," it said. "Call me tonight. No time is too late. I never sleep."

Wood rose, put on shorts and a shirt and filled a glass with guava nectar. He drank it, standing by his open window, feeling the breeze. Then he lay down again.

But sleep wouldn't return. He shifted in bed, trying to turn his mind off. Finally, at 4 a.m., he gave up. He swung his legs down, righted himself at the edge of the mattress and turned on the bed lamp. His phone was on the nightstand. He stared at it for what seemed a long time. Then he made the call. Papaya picked up on the first ring.

"Wood? Are you there?"

He started to speak, but there was a click and the line went dead. He glared at the phone, imagining it had a mind of its own. A devious mind. He lifted his legs onto the mattress and stretched out, setting the phone back on the nightstand.

Twenty minutes later it rang.

"You again," Wood said.

"I'm sorry. I was undressing. I'm naked now," she said. "I'm going to curl up in bed and talk to you."

"I should warn you."

"About what?"

"I'm involved with someone."

"Aren't we all," Papaya laughed. "Where are you?"

"In bed."

"On the Key?"

"Mm-hmm. Where are you?"

"Buenos Aires. I've been reading your book."

"What do you think?"

"You're a smart man, writing for the hopeful ones."

"My readers are hopeful?"

"Aren't they? They're not like me. Or you."

At the party, he had told her he was separated, living alone. Now she wanted to hear about the women he'd met.

Wood declined. "I'm not going to do that."

"You can tell me," she said. "I won't be jealous."

He was silent. Papaya waited. Finally he dropped his guard.

He talked about Callie and Tamarind, about Mamey and Piña and Pumelo. He didn't mention Gwen. The conversation was relaxed, fluid and easy, not what he had expected.

"Love is impossible." Papaya sighed. "I just ended things with a woman. Lately, I'm so distrustful of men— All men. Not just you."

She spoke with a lilt, confidential, vulnerable.

"I didn't say goodbye at the party." Wood took a breath. "You seemed to be fading on me."

And then, without thinking, he crossed the line.

"I wanted to see you again." His tone was resigned, recognizing the distance.

"That's not so hard," she said. "I'll be back the last day of the Fest. I can't miss the madness."

Silence. Wood held his breath, thinking of Gwen.

"Can I stay with you?" Papaya asked.

"You don't have a place on the Key?"

"I'm not permanent anywhere," Papaya said. "Maybe someday. With the right man."

7

Wood received a message from Gwen the next morning. "Call me," it said. And he was going to, but he'd overslept and didn't want to bother her at work. Groceries and laundry consumed him till noon. "Let's talk tonight," he texted her. Then he went wandering.

There were more visitors on the street than the day before. He saw excitement in their eyes and anticipation; nothing reckless or unruly, but they weren't yet masked or painted, they weren't naked or drunk or high.

Before he knew it, the sun had descended. Gwen's workday had ended. She was at home, relaxing, fixing something to eat. He was getting hungry himself.

He stopped in front of one eatery and another, eyeing the menus posted outside. A Cuban place struck his fancy, and the prices were reasonable. He peered through the blinds, seeing no one he recognized inside. So he stepped through the entrance, up to the register, and ordered roasted pork with rice and beans to go.

When he returned to his apartment, he was no longer hungry. So he put the pork in the refrigerator and collapsed on the sofa. Their time together had been so intense, he knew Gwen would understand. He needed some sleep. First thing tomorrow, he thought.

He woke at 5 a.m. There was a message from Gwen from the previous evening, expressing concern. Was he alright? He was going to text her, but he fell back asleep with the phone in his hand. He rose five hours later, but by then Gwen was at work.

I'll call her this afternoon, he thought.

But when midday arrived, it was Piña he called. She was still his friend, and he cared about her too. When she picked up, he greeted her with affection.

"Greentop," he said.

"That was quick," she laughed. "What is it?"

"I want to see you."

"When?"

"Tonight. Right now."

"I'm putting some ferns on a kitty. Everything alright?"

He met her at Refugio. Mango was behind the bar. Wood ordered blushes.

"How's Gwen?" Piña wondered.

"She had to work late. Have your pipe with you?"

Piña regarded him, then shook her head.

He put his lips to her ear. "Yes you do. Let's see how high we can get."

She laughed. When they'd downed the blushes, they had another pair, and another. Then they stumbled to her car, and she drove to Stock Island. On the way, Wood thought about Gwen. She'd forgive his silence. Things had happened so quickly. He needed a little time to himself.

Stubby had left some Turkish hash in the trailer. They sat on Piña's bed and smoked it. Wood turned to the drawing of the interlocked crocs on the wall.

"Are they fighting or screwing?"

"I told you, they're screwing."

"Strong stuff," he said.

"Have some more."

"The drawing, I mean."

"I'm going to put those crocs on your chest," she said. "Here." She traced a circle, squinting to see through his shirt. "I'll make your nipple his eye. You won't feel a thing. We'll get you high."

"Hard to remove, if I changed my mind."

"Impossible," Piña smiled. "Have a look." She reached under the bed and pulled out a sheaf of drawings.

"You did these?" He turned the pages.

"Sure."

Wood raised his head. "Do you think about the future?"

"Not much."

"Neither do I. We're similar that way." He raised his forefinger as if making a point. Then he touched the tip of her nose.

"Careful," Piña said. She drew on the pipe.

"I was being affectionate."

She squinched her eyes. "Are things okay with Gwen?"

"Absolutely."

"She's committed? You're really her guy?"

He nodded. "Toujours, she says. Forever."

Piña passed him the pipe. "Maybe she wants your name on her back."

During the next two days, visitors arrived in droves. The first costumes appeared, along with some thongs and naked breasts. At midday on lower Duval, drunks staggered among the sober, and there were overt displays, with noise from cars and motorcycles—revving, honking and loud music.

Wood ambled through the crowds, losing himself, downing blushes and talking to strangers. At midnight, he stood in the surf at South Beach and let the milkshake loosen his knees while he gazed at the stars. He hadn't called Gwen or replied to her messages, but she understood. Only a few days had passed since they'd spoken.

He wanted to make good on his promise to Callie, so he invited her out.

When she answered the door, she looked taxed and scornful. But she was wearing a flattering outfit. Her face was made up, and there wasn't a hair out of place. "I have a right to be angry," she said. "You're the father of three."

They started with blushes, then Callie wanted a cortadito,

so they stopped at a Cuban cafe she liked. Wood had two, and the caffeine locked his jaw and made his hands shake. They walked the harbor with a loud mob. More were painted and in costume now. Where the day boats docked, they saw fishermen cleaning their haul, while pelicans competed for scraps. Like Piña, Callie wanted to know about Gwen. "What makes her so special?" Wood didn't answer. Every time Callie returned to the attack, he changed the subject. She had a show that evening, so they headed for Hao Zhidao before the sun set.

As they entered, Wood saw Tamarind wave to him from a corner booth. He stepped over to say hello and introduced Callie. Guava was on duty, so the service was impeccable. But when she brought the check and the cookie, her expression was grave.

"Don't I get one?" Callie protested.

Guava ignored her, posting herself by Wood's side.

He looked at Guava, then he broke the cookie's wings.

TO ONE WHO WAITS, the fortune said, A MOMENT SEEMS A YEAR.

I'll call her as soon as I take Callie home, Wood thought.

But he didn't.

The first week of silence ended, and the second began.

Wood's eclipse was an accident. Unintentional. He loved Gwen. They had a future together. But he hadn't responded to her messages, and the messages had ceased.

It was late at night, and Wood was sleeping.

Suddenly, he was wide awake. He sat up, every muscle

tense, as if an alarm had sounded and his life depended on immediate action.

Josu, he thought. He'd been dreaming of Gwen's husband. Josu was standing naked beneath a papaya tree, his black skin gleaming. The fruit that hung from the branches was already halved, ready to eat. Gwen was out of sight, but Wood could hear her voice. Was she talking to Josu or to him? "I couldn't let go," she said.

Wood rose, found his phone and called Tray. His heart was racing, his face beaded with sweat.

"Man," Tray said, "it's still dark outside. What is it?"

"I have to see you. Right now. I'm coming over."

When Wood arrived, Tray was in shorts and an undershirt. "Bijou's asleep," he said, motioning Wood upstairs to the den on the second floor.

"I've fucked things up," Wood started.

"Sit down."

"I've left Gwen for dead."

"What?"

"I haven't seen her. Or spoken to her."

Tray sank into an armchair. "Why not?"

"I don't know."

"How long has it been?"

"Eight days. I'm going to send her flowers. Lilies. A whole armful, with a note begging her to forgive me."

"What happened, before you went silent?"

Wood told him about "cozy" and the dinner at Ten One Five. He repeated what Gwen had said about having children and building a life together. "I'm single now. Enjoying my freedom. Maybe part of me doesn't want to be pinned down."

"Maybe her expression of need frightened you." Tray shook his head. "This feels like fear to me. Or revenge."

"What?"

"By being absent," Tray said, "you're doing to Gwen what was done to you."

Wood frowned. "By Vadette?"

"Or by your mother," Tray said. "You have to talk to Gwen."

"Lilies," Wood said, "and a long note. I'll beg her to cook dinner."

"However you do it, break the silence. Don't wait."

Back in his apartment, Wood sat down to compose the note. It went slowly. The begging and pleading was easy, and so was the self-abasement. The explaining was harder. The reasons he came up with at first were practical. Those weren't credible. He struggled to describe what had been in his heart, and the harder he tried, the more confusing the letter got. Finally he took a break. It was light outside and there were cars in the street.

Wood checked the time. 10 a.m. A walk around the block, to untangle his thoughts. He was headed for the door when his phone rang.

It was Papaya.

"I'm here," she said. "Do I have the right address?" She rattled off the number and street.

Wood was speechless.

"I'm coming over," Papaya said.

"When?"

"Right now."

"You're crazy," he said. But the line was already dead.

His apartment was a mess. He turned on the kitchen tap, then he hurried into the bathroom to shave. A moment later he put down the razor and grabbed his phone. "Don't come," he texted. "I don't want to see you." He stared at himself in the mirror. "Fuck." His lips hardened, then he lifted the razor and continued shaving.

When he glanced out the window, he saw a white sedan pulling up. The rear door opened and Papaya stepped out. Footfalls on the stair, then a loud knock, and the next thing he knew, she was standing on the threshold unmasked—platinum hair, icy eyes, her breasts so pointed they might have been turned on a lathe.

"Well—" Papaya laughed.

To Wood's surprise, there was a woman at her hip, tall and grave. Papaya faced her. "I'll get myself ready. He'll help you unload the car."

Papaya stepped past him, into the apartment.

The tall woman extended her hand. "I'm Okra," she said.

"Wait a minute." He raised his hands.

Papaya turned full around, hair sweeping like a dancer's skirt. "You knew I'd come." She eyed him sidelong, as if they shared some bosom secret.

Wood laughed. "I did?"

The sedan was crammed with luggage. Together, he and Okra hauled the suitcases and carryalls up the stairs. Okra was lanky and her cheeks were hollow, as if the cheer had been sucked out of her head. Papaya retreated to the bedroom and closed the door. Wood heard the shower running.

Okra opened the bags and piled clothing and costumery on the sofa and chairs. When there was no more space, she used the floor. "Can I help?" Wood asked. Okra shook her head.

She dragged a large suitcase into the kitchen and began unloading it, stacking jars on the counter. Sacks of tubes followed, rags and sponges, spray nozzles and brushes, beads, feathers and appliqué. The bedroom door opened, and when Wood turned, he saw Papaya stark naked, her hair bound in a towel. She stepped through the piles of clothing toward him.

Wood stared at her. "Do you mind telling me what's going on?"

"You have a disguise?" Papaya asked.

"Costume," Okra corrected. She was opening tubes and uncapping jars. Wood saw her select a brush.

"We brought some things for you," Papaya said.

Two hours later, a large open mouth with scarlet lips covered Papaya's front. The upper lip crossed her sternum, and the lower crossed her hips. Between, the gaping orifice was a night filled with stars.

"What do you think?" Papaya asked.

Wood regarded the dark sky over her heart and innards.

"My hand would pass through you," he said.

"You're staring."

Papaya's nipples were visible beneath the paint. "You're naked," he said, grasping her shoulder.

Her incisors met and she spoke between them. "Don't smudge me."

"Why are you here? What do you want?"

Her eyes softened, yielding. "Be crazy with me."

Okra emerged from the kitchen wearing a cream-colored bikini and a cape with green sequins. She handed Papaya a mask, the same one she'd worn at the party.

Papaya put the mask on. "Now," she smiled, "we'll fix you up. Where are those cowboy boots?"

"In the bedroom."

Papaya motioned and Okra went looking.

"Take your clothes off," Papaya said.

He met her gaze, mistrustful, unwilling.

Papaya took his hand and put his fingers on her nipple. "That's what I want."

He looked like a circus act, in white tights and a tutu of pink chiffon. He was bare-chested, but there were star-shaped pasties on his nipples, and a white feather boa around his shoulders. The boots were on his feet, and a pink cowboy hat was on his head. Okra had painted his lips and covered his cheeks with blush.

He'd argued, but Papaya insisted. "It's part of the Fest," she said. "Just play along." As they approached the Angela intersection, a mob of people appeared in the street, all wearing tutus.

"See," Papaya said. "Time for Wood's medicine."

Okra halted. She was carrying a coiled rope over her shoulder. She retrieved a pill and handed it to him.

"What is it?" he asked.

Papaya waved his question away and stepped closer. "Take a drink from me."

He frowned.

"Run your tongue under mine," she said. "Juice will come out."

He peered into her unreadable eyes.

"Hurry up."

Wood covered her mouth with his own and slid his tongue beneath hers. Saliva pooled around her teeth. He sucked at the liquid, popped the pill and swallowed it.

They continued down the street, and as they joined the

mob, his self-consciousness faded. The men were all wearing tutus and garish costumes. A group nearby were dressed like bees, striped yellow and black, with wings on their backs. The women were dressed or painted like fruit, laced with leaves or spattered with seeds. Faces turned and stared at Papaya. She was posturing, waving, talking loudly to one and another.

"Put your mask on," Okra said.

He raised the mask from around his neck and slid it over his eyes.

Sirens sounded. A pair of motorcycle policeman led the mob onto Duval. The Tutu March was starting.

"Have fun," Okra said.

Wood stepped forward with the crowd, scanning the faces that watched from the sidewalks, worried he'd be seen by someone he knew. Gwen avoided the Fest, but what if—

Papaya and Okra waved, keeping pace with him. He waved back, trying to relax. What was the harm? Papaya was right. It was all in fun. Men in tutus sashayed ahead and on either side, aping a female gait, enjoying themselves. "Like this," Papaya shouted, swaying her hips. Pennons of hair floated and sank with her camping stride. Wood followed her example.

A gay couple strolled beside him, one in a black tutu with thigh-high boots, the other in a white one with ballerina slippers. Up ahead, Wood saw someone of uncertain gender with a tutu of fresh bananas, and another with a jester's mask, waving a magic wand. The jester had a wide lipstick grin and pink petals curling from his head. Wood thought of the Magus.

Onlookers milled on either side of Duval, drinking, shouting and taking pictures. Some wore costumes, others were naked and painted, following the theme. There were fruits of every description, farmers and pickers, and a man in a crop-dusting costume, with wings of paper-mâché and a propeller on his head.

Papaya had stopped to pose for photos. Men crowded around her. Did they suspect who she was? A moment later, she and Okra were waving and hurrying to catch up. Life was a Fest, Wood thought, and he was playing along. He didn't know where he was going, but things would work out.

At the end of Duval, the March dissolved.

"That's it," Okra said, grabbing his elbow.

"What's next?"

"The Pet Show," she said, passing the coiled rope to Papaya.

The two women escorted him to a club on the corner, where men from the Tutu March were being led across a stage on all fours. Papaya stopped and ran the rope around his neck.

"No thanks." Wood pushed her away.

"Don't be like that," she laughed. "I want to show you off."

"Wood?" A costumed woman stopped before him.

He froze, fearful. He opened his mouth, but nothing came out.

"Fig," the woman said.

"How are you?" He nodded, trying to smile. She was wearing a corset, and what looked like a large bug was painted around her neck, its wings spanning her shoulders.

"It's a fig wasp," she said.

"You again." Papaya eyed Fig with distaste.

"The phony," Fig snarled back, and she tromped away.

Wood squinted at Papaya. "Clip your nails."

"What's her name," she demanded, "this woman you're 'involved with'? You're afraid she'll see you with me, aren't you."

He set his jaw, feeling like a fool.

Papaya tugged on the rope.

"I said no."

"Please," she implored. "Just for today. Pretend you belong to me."

She embraced him, and Wood felt her breasts touch his chest.

"We're having fun," she whispered, "aren't we?"

"We are," he said. "But I'm not your dog."

The man on stage had crouched on his haunches. The woman ordered him to beg, and when he did, she hooked her thumb in her thong and lowered it as a reward. The crowd whistled and raised their cups, cheering the performance.

Okra removed the leash, and three of them continued down Duval, weaving through bars. There was a party in each—a Pink party, an Underwear party, an Egg-Eating party.

"The Pepper party," Papaya shouted, pulling Wood into a club with red neon walls. The tables were covered with paper cups. She grabbed two and passed one to him. It was filled with rust-colored liquid.

"Chug it," she said.

Wood raised the cup and downed the contents. It ravaged his throat, and his lungs filled with smoke. Hornets buzzed in his ears, and the earth beneath him began to shake. Papaya had swallowed hers. She dropped the cup and her eyes blistered. She raised her hands and combed her temples, and her hair tendriled like a silver medusa.

"You're crazy," he gasped.

"Crazy—" She choked, falling against him. "Crazy for *you*. Can't you see?"

They stumbled back onto the sidewalk. A ukulele band was coming down the street.

It had been only hours, but it felt to Wood like days had passed. The pill Okra had given him turned the sky dark; the street looked like Duval, but it had rolled itself out in a different world—a world peopled with alien creatures. Their costumes were gone. He was seeing their real natures.

Papaya flew ahead, around the corner and up a side street. Wood followed, with Okra beside him. They were approaching a theater. "Stages," the lit sign read.

There was a crowd in front. Papaya waved to him and pushed through them. When the three reached the lobby, she retrieved tickets from a wallet that hung from Okra's waist, and they were escorted to a table up front. The theater was packed. They sat down, and a few moments later, the house lights dimmed.

A blare of trumpets, and a woman dressed like a schoolgirl skipped to center stage and held up a large placard: *Presenting: The Story of Wood.*

He turned. "What is this?"

"I thought you'd like it," Papaya smiled.

The schoolgirl skipped off, and a man wandered onto the stage, lit by a lone spot. He was tall and dark, broad in the shoulders with narrow hips and slender legs.

"I'm a pilgrim," the man said, reflecting out loud, "and I'm far from home. I was starved in my native land. I've traveled countless miles, hoping for better, but no relief have I found." He put his hands on his middle. "Have pity on me."

He spread his arms and launched into a song that described his malnourished condition.

"I feel for him." Papaya thumped her breast and cackled.

As the song ended, a second figure appeared on the other side of the stage, pink from top to bottom, with a snaking tail and a head like a donkey's. Its ears stood straight up, and its triangular wings batted behind, as if it had just come down from the sky.

"Who is that?" Wood grabbed Papaya's shoulder.

She shook her head.

He looked at Okra. "Do you know who that is?"

"Quiet," a man barked from a table nearby.

"I can help you," the pink creature offered, extending its arm to the Pilgrim.

Wood saw the actor's eyes through the donkey headdress. As the pink creature crossed the stage, the eyes shifted. The man or woman inside was scouting the audience. In a voice high but gruff, the actor burst into song, lauding itself, calling itself the Pilgrim's salvation. "There's a farm just around the bend," the pink creature sang. "Let's inquire there."

The curtains opened on a clutter of pasteboard buildings and a giant tree center stage, with large colored objects hanging from its branches. A man with a straw hat and overalls was hoeing around the tree, while two teenage boys and two girls sowed seeds behind him.

The pink creature strode up to the farmer. "Excuse me."

The farmer straightened and put his hand to his back with a groan.

"This poor fellow," the pink creature slapped the Pilgrim's back, "is starving. Will you feed him?"

The farmer glanced at the tree and shook his head. "The growing season is almost over, but I'm not going to harvest yet."

"Make today the day," the pink creature cried, and he turned, raising his arms to the audience, urging them all to join in.

The crowd obliged. "Come on. Pull them down. Pick 'em already. What are you waiting for?" They clapped and whistled, and the farmer's resistance was overcome.

"Well," he allowed, "maybe just one."

"Let's go," Wood whispered to Papaya. He had no desire to see himself dissected in public.

"I want to know what happens to him," she said.

One of the farmer's sons was climbing the tree. He shook a low limb, and a large hanging fruit, a purple caimito, came loose and fell to the stage. As the Pilgrim approached it, the caimito uncurled.

It was a woman in a purple gown, and when the Pilgrim explained his hunger, she burst into song, opening her gown to reveal a white bodice and frilled panties.

"Can I eat her?" the Pilgrim asked.

"She's not quite ready," the pink creature faced the house. "The louder you are, the riper she gets."

With that, a wave of shouts and whistles rose from the crowd.

"Burlesque," Papaya laughed.

The caimito woman sang while she peeled off her gloves. The crowd hooted and whistled, and the woman unlaced her bodice and removed her panties. When she was down to a G-string and pasties, the farmer's children carried a giant straw from the barn. The caimito woman hugged the straw, and the Pilgrim sucked, feeding himself as she sang a last chorus. Then she sighed and fell to the stage, consumed.

Restored by the feeding, the Pilgrim did a comical song while he circled the tree and hopped on one leg.

Wood gripped Papaya's arm. "That's enough."

"Quiet," she snapped.

"I'm still hungry," the Pilgrim told the farmer. And with the help of the clamoring crowd, the farmer was again persuaded. One by one, shaking the branches, using ladders and poles, his children brought the hanging fruits down. Each was a different woman, and when the woman had removed her clothing and sung her song, the Pilgrim used the straw to refresh himself.

Finally the tree was empty. No fruits remained.

"What a wondrous bounty," the pink creature lauded the farmer. "I can only imagine, the labors through spring and summer, the great pains you and your family took—"

"I'm not full," the Pilgrim said.

"You've eaten them all," the farmer told him.

"Every last one," the pink creature agreed.

"You're wrong." The Pilgrim pointed. "The best is still on the tree. The papaya."

"You're imagining things." The farmer shook his head.

"I'm looking right at her," the Pilgrim insisted.

"Papaya's a myth," the farmer said.

The chair legs beside Wood grunted.

"Get her down," the Pilgrim exclaimed. "I want her, I tell you."

A drumroll sounded. The pink creature turned toward the audience. As Wood watched, the eyes inside the headdress fixed on him.

"Don't let this poor fellow make a fool of himself," the farmer cried.

"How dare you," Papaya shouted, rising to her feet.

The actors froze.

Papaya climbed onto the table and faced them. "What do you know?" she raged.

The theater was silent.

Papaya turned her back to the stage and strode from one tabletop to another, kicking drinks over. She leaped from the last and disappeared through the double doors. Wood and Okra hurried after her, through the lobby and into the street.

She halted amid the revelers, eyes shut, hands covering her ears. Okra reached her and put her arms around her. Papaya's chest was heaving.

As Wood approached, she opened her eyes and stared at him. Then she shrugged Okra loose. "We're going to Cowboy Jack's," Papaya said, and she headed down Duval, shouldering her way through the crowd.

A strange woman, Wood thought, *and a strange night.* The Fest was speaking to him, but what was it saying? As Papaya moved, her eyes darted, watching for threats, alert to things at eye level, and above and below as well, as if she feared the earth might crack or an enemy might descend from the sky.

Cowboy Jack's was the largest club on the Key. As they entered, the space opened around them, with seating on multiple levels. The place was packed. At its center was a pen, and inside the pen a mechanical bull was bucking. The woman riding it was naked and painted, and she gripped the pommel with both hands. Papaya pushed her way forward, Wood and Okra followed.

As they reached the guard gate, the rider was thrown. She shook her head and picked herself up. The pen's walls and floor were rubberized, inflated with air. The buzzer sounded and the bull rattled to rest.

Papaya waved to the bull tender. She drew up beside him, and when he leaned toward her, she put her lips to his ear. Then she turned to Wood, took the hat from his head and set it on hers. She pulled the white boa from his neck, wrapped it around her own and nodded to the tender. He laughed and opened the guard gate.

Papaya entered the pen and marched toward the bull. Wood looked at Okra. Her eyes were wide.

As they watched, Papaya climbed onto the beast, wrapped her thighs around its flanks, adjusted her mask and put her feet in the stirrups. The crowd noise mounted. Wood saw the tender grip the control box lever.

The movement was modest at first, the bull's rear end rising and plunging in slow motion. It swiveled around. Papaya pointed at the crowd, smiling as if she recognized faces. Was that for show? Did anyone know who she was?

The tender pushed the lever forward.

Papaya arched her back and raised one arm, and the beast erupted beneath her. She was flying, spine buckling, head jerking. Cheers, shouts, whistles. She dug her heels into the bull's metal flanks, and the crowd noise grew. Okra grabbed Wood's shoulder, pale and mute.

"Is that who I think it is?" a drunk lisped in Wood's ear.

It seemed she'd be thrown at any moment, but Papaya kept her seat. Her command was a thrill to watch. With her free hand, she pulled the boa from her neck, whipped the bull's rump and sent the boa flying. She grabbed the pink hat and sailed it into the crowd. The next instant, the buzzer sounded; and an instant after that, she was airborne.

Her side struck the wall of the pen, and she landed facedown on its floor. She lay still for a moment, then raised herself, arms spread, accepting the cheers as she staggered back through the gate.

Wood embraced her. She was breathless, sweating.

"You're next," she said. "I'm going to do that to you." She put her lips over his, and the crowd roared.

"My apartment," he said.

"We can't miss the parade." Papaya grabbed his hand and led the way out of Cowboy Jack's and into the street, with Okra behind.

"Aye, aye. Wait." The lisping drunk staggered after them.

Papaya looked over her shoulder, and the fear Wood saw in her eyes made him shiver. Was this what it meant to be desired by so many? She was like a hunted animal.

"Aye—" The drunk was waving and shouting. "Fiskey. Geezus. Mel," he cried.

Papaya turned down an alley and entered a paved courtyard. Beneath strings of outdoor lights, Wood saw a pair of large pools and a crowd of people in and around them, naked. Some were having sex, and the rest looked about to join in.

A big man waved Okra toward him. She glanced at Papaya.

The masked woman reached for Okra's neck, and the green cape fell to the paving, glittering around their feet like a puddle of slime. She untied Okra's bikini and pushed her into the big man's arms. "Go on," Papaya said.

Then she grabbed Wood's hand and led him between the pools and up a stairway to a balcony overlooking Duval.

The street had been cleared. There were barricades along both curbs, and between the storefronts and the barricades, people were swarming. A squadron of motorcycle cops approached from lower Duval, sirens yawping, blue lights flashing. Then the first float appeared.

A giant inflated infant lay on its back in a crib of trees, while fountains of fruit juice rose around it, raining on the doting parents standing beneath. It was sponsored by the Key West baby store.

Next was a float from a local bar, with rowdy patrons covered in goop, throwing fruit at each other. Then came drum majorettes and a marching band playing their school anthem, "Squeeze 'Em Dry for Key West High."

Wood put his hand on Papaya's waist. A sconce behind them lit her platinum waves and the bridge of her nose. He thought of Gwen.

"We belong together," Papaya said.

They stared at each other without speaking. Then she closed her eyes and offered her lips. Confetti fell from the windows like snow. As Wood kissed her, the crowd noise rose like a storm, whistling, shouting, screaming.

Papaya laughed and pointed. A float from the local hospital was passing. Patients in beds were getting intravenous injections of fruit juice from topless nurses. Beside the float, doctors walked in surgical scrubs. Each held a tank in one hand and a nozzle in the other, spraying juice on the crowd.

A troupe of gay men in thongs and capes performed "Dance of the Fruit Flies" to chamber music. A float with a giant pie followed, sponsored by a local bakery. The pie had "Eat Me" scribed on its top, and as it passed, revelers in lime pajamas jumped out.

Last was the royal float. A couple had been coronated for the Fest, and they appeared now on the quarterdeck of a lavish ship. Papaya laughed. The ship was a giant halved fruit—*la fruta suprema*. The royal couple stood by their thrones, throwing seeds at the crowd. The king wore a cowboy hat, and the queen wore a crown.

Papaya removed her mask. The ice in her eyes had melted. Wood saw yearning in them, and deep desire.

"They're imposters," she said. "You're fantasy's king. And I'm its queen."

They climbed the stairs of his apartment in the dark. Okra was huddled on the second-floor landing. Wood roused her and helped her inside.

The front room was hot and humid. The air conditioning had failed while they were gone, and the apartment was like a sauna.

Papaya escorted Okra to the bathroom and closed the door.

They returned a few minutes later. Okra was wearing a

robe. Papaya, still naked and painted, explained that she would sleep on his bed with him. Okra would sleep on the sofa. Wood nodded, wondering what she was thinking.

Okra collapsed on the sofa. Papaya stepped into the bedroom. He followed.

Wood stood watching while she stripped off the sheets and blankets, turned off the lights and stretched out on the bed. He removed his briefs and boots, and sat beside her. He could feel Gwen's presence hovering around him. Some things could not be forgiven.

He put his hand on Papaya's thigh.

"You're crazy." She spoke the words fondly, but she pushed his hand away.

"I want you."

"No." Her tone was brittle.

"You were going to ride me like that bull."

"Not tonight," she said.

She sounded piqued. Tense. Angry. What had happened? Wood sat there in the sweltering darkness, galled and confused. Finally he lay down.

There was no hope of sleep. Papaya's naked body was six inches away. He could smell her skin and her hair, and the moonlight filtering through the drapes edged her curves. He could see her turning and twisting, sweat threading her thighs, beaded on her breasts. Gwen came to mind again. The memories made him sick. The armful of lilies was impossibly distant, as was the note he'd tried to compose.

The heat was unbearable. He couldn't stop shifting. Finally Papaya lay still. Was she asleep or awake? He extended his hand and touched her ribcage. Still as a corpse. Sometime later, he drifted into a dream or a waking night fever.

He was on the bed alone. The woman who'd been sleeping beside him had risen. She was in the bathroom, and she'd left the door ajar. He could hear her urinating. A moment later, she turned on the shower.

In his fever, Wood rose. Through the crack in the bathroom doorway, he could see the steam coiling around her. The hot water was washing away her body paint, and the cover of flesh as well. Her wet back gleamed like an exoskeleton. Her disguise was dissolving. He could see her as she really was now—eight legs crimped against her trunk, clawed arms raised, tail curled up her backside. She was standing on the tile beneath the spray, but she could have been climbing the wall or crossing the ceiling.

At six in the morning, Wood woke. He put on a t-shirt and shorts and crept out of the building. He walked to the lighthouse through a gray fog, and with each step, his fury mounted. Papaya was deranged, devious and cold-blooded, completely uncaring. Why was he gambling his future with someone like that?

The two women woke at noon. Wood was in the front room, writing in his logbook. Papaya entered, wearing a blouse and short skirt. She approached slowly, as if she could sense his spite. When she reached his side, she stood quietly. Wood ignored her.

"I'm sorry," she said, "I came to see you. The Fest was just an excuse."

He heard her words, but he didn't believe them.

"Please," she said.

Wood looked up. Her blue eyes were brimming with guilt, like a criminal expecting a harsh sentence.

"Let's spend the afternoon together," Papaya said. "Okra can be on her own."

He didn't respond.

She proposed a couple of things, then she stopped herself. "No. You decide."

Wood could feel the manipulation in her voice, and he could see it in her eyes. When he stood, they flared, fearful, innocent, as if she feared some violence. Then she laughed.

He laughed back—at her, not with her.

"I make things so hard," she said. "You're right to be angry. What can I do? I want to be with you. I don't want to go."

Wood stared at her, wishing they'd never met. Then he drew a deep breath and relented. He suggested Taylor Beach, to get the breeze from the sea.

She had him drive the sedan she'd rented. Around Duval, the cleanup had started. Workers loaded dumpsters with trash, while forklifts hauled barricades to waiting trucks.

Papaya seemed not to notice. She stared at the dash and

spoke to herself. Her words seemed like whimsy at first, then Wood got the drift. She was opening a window for him, giving him a view inside her head.

"He thinks I'm angry," she said. "I'm going to ignore him. Pretend he doesn't exist." She laughed. "That's not going to work. I want him so badly. Last night—" She sighed. "I had to hold myself back."

She smiled to herself. Wood distrusted that smile and everything she said.

When they arrived at the beach, she was still rambling. As they walked through the pines, her banter grew stranger.

"Feed him," she said. "Shock him, then starve him. Let him search his cage. Put a pellet where he can smell it, outside his door."

Were her moods just fakery? Did she plan every switch and snub in advance? Why was she painting herself as a hellcat now? Was she going to give him the upper hand, or was it just another way to tempt him?

They reached the sand. Papaya was talking about sex now. "I want it," she said. "He's no fool. He can see how hot I am." She fanned the air in front of her skirt. "One word, one look—"

Wood halted. "Is there anything I could do that would please you?" he snarled.

"There's a place a few minutes east of here where you can jump off a bridge."

He grabbed her silver locks and twisted them. The other hand hooked her neckline, yanking it down, exposing her breast. Papaya roared with indignation and swung, striking his face with her fist.

His arms fell. He took a step back.

She burst out laughing.

"You've done it," he gasped. "You've figured me out. You're what I want: illusions, fantasies; lies, with more lies hidden beneath."

Her laugh turned into a wicked smile. She straightened her blouse.

"You're a mystery with dozens of clues," Wood said, "but none of them add up. You're like a bad story."

"I'm a terrible story." Her smile vanished. "I'm *your* story, Wood. The story of love you're afraid to tell." Her chest heaved, her head bowed and she began to sob. "I'm trying to be honest." She raised her fists to her temples and shook them. "Trying, trying— Can't you see? We're the same. We have the same fears, we know the same pain. We can't feel love the way most people do."

"That's *your* story."

"Now who's pretending?" Papaya drew closer. Her eyes were piercing. "I know who you are."

Wood felt the naked contact again—secret, harrowing—unlike anything he'd felt with Gwen or anyone else. Papaya's lips were inches from his.

"Why did you refuse me last night?" he hissed.

"I was afraid."

"Of what?"

"The woman you're with."

Wood's breath stopped. He drew back, seeing the turquoise water over her shoulder. *Why here?* he thought. Why had he taken Papaya to the place he'd met Gwen? Did he imagine Gwen's presence would somehow protect him? Or was he turning Gwen's power over to her?

"What's her name?" Papaya asked.

All at once, he knew why he'd faded on Gwen. What she wanted, he couldn't give her. "Gwen," he murmured. "Her name is Gwen."

"I hate this," Papaya said. "Why can't I come out and say it? I'm mad for you. I have to have you. Are you listening?"

"I'm listening."

"The games— They have to end. You and I— That's all that matters." She put her hand on his chest. "You know my history. I've been a symbol of love for many men. But— Only one can give Papaya what she needs."

He met her desperate eyes.

"You know what I'm feeling," she said. "You feel it too."

"I feel it," he nodded. "I felt it the night we met."

"I'm leaving at six for Havana," she said. "Join me there. We'll start life over. Just the two of us."

8

Mamey ran the cutter over the box's top, opened its corrugated wings and began piling custard apples in the space between mangos and figs. She noticed a woman standing beside the coconuts. Her hair was braided and bound around her head.

The woman stepped forward. Stray locks dangled by her ears. Mamey recognized her features and her graceful carriage.

"It's so cheery here," Gwen greeted her.

"Always," Mamey said.

"You remember me?"

"Of course."

"The bright colors, the wonderful scents—"

Mamey slid the cutter into her apron pocket. There were shadows under Gwen's green eyes, and her smile was false as a clown's.

"Can I help you with anything?" Mamey asked.

Gwen's lips parted. Then she sighed. "Probably not."

"How are things with Wood?"

"Not well, I'm afraid."

Mamey stepped closer. "The last I heard—"

Gwen's lips trembled. She was on the verge of tears.

Mamey put her arm around Gwen's shoulders. "It's early. Business is light."

The crowds were dwindling. The pace of the Key was returning to normal.

"There's a table at the back," Mamey said. "Would you like to talk?"

Tray settled himself on the seat at Hao Zhidao.

"How's business?" Wood asked.

Tray shrugged. "Two fighting couples and a sex change pre-op. He wants to get his dick cut off, and I have to certify that he's mentally stable. Nice guy. Six-four, with large implants. He leads diving tours to the Dry Tortugas."

"What will they do to him?"

"Cut it off, turn it inside out and make a vagina out of it." Tray sighed. "It won't end well. He'll never pass as a woman. What's new? You sounded stressed on the phone."

Wood nodded. "A lot's happened."

He told Tray about Papaya's visit and the invitation to Havana.

Tray was stunned. "What about Gwen?"

"I love Gwen," Wood said. "Papaya is a devil. But she understands me."

Guava approached.

"Subgum Wonton," Wood told her.

"I'll have the Crystal Prawns," Tray said.

Guava penciled her ideographs and stepped away.

"With Gwen," Wood said, "it was never right. It's too late now. She'll forget me."

Tray was silent.

"You could be happy for me," Wood said. "Who ever thought I'd end up with Papaya?"

"What is it you see in her?" Tray asked.

"She's bigger than life. There's magic with Papaya, a mystery that will never be solved and will never grow old."

"If I was a woman," Tray said, "and I was attracted to a man who thought that the essence of desire was mystery, I'd worry that if I fully revealed myself, it would destroy his desire. I would guard my secrets, to keep the magic alive for him."

"She's opening up." Wood smiled.

"You want a shrink's view?"

"Sure."

"A man falls in love with a mysterious woman, someone he's heard is unattainable. That tells me that the man is a child inside."

"A child." Wood cocked his head.

"Our sense of mystery and wonder starts in infancy. The mother is a wondrous presence, and a kindly one. But she frightens us too. She's powerful. Mysterious. Her love can be offered or taken away at a moment's notice, without explanation. A man who believes that's how women are—or should be—is seeing them through an infant's eyes."

"Papaya's my mother," Wood said.

"The mother you couldn't have. Or didn't want. Whoever this woman is—"

"Please, don't start that."

"She sees your weakness, and she's using it against you. You wouldn't be at her mercy if she was a real woman. She'd be depending on you as much as you depend on her." Tray's voice grew hushed. "You're playing a dangerous game."

"You're worried about me."

"I am. You're giving her all this power. What if she drives you over the brink— If she says, 'shove off,' and what you hear is, 'Wood, my son, I don't give a damn about you—' What then? I can't imagine anything worse."

Wood considered Tray's words. "Here comes the food."

When they had finished the meal, Guava brought the check and two cookies.

"What's this?" Wood regarded her.

"Tonight, a second is needed." She extended her tray.

Wood took a cookie and cracked it open. "ONLY TEARS CAN BRING THE DREAMER BACK TO EARTH," he read.

Guava looked regretful. She pursed her lips.

Tray picked up the remaining cookie. He broke it in two, stared at the fortune and passed it to Wood as Guava stepped away.

"A SMALL GIFT COULD MEAN A LOT TO SOMEONE," Wood read.

"That's Bijou." Tray drew a breath. "Things have been rocky lately."

"Oh no. Not you."

"She's given me an ultimatum," Tray said.

"You can't lose her."

"No, I can't."

Wood set Tray's fortune down. "Maybe it's time to convert to the 'religion of us.' Say a prayer and buy her a ring." He laughed. "Any more advice you'd like to share?"

"You're hurting her," Mamey said.

Wood closed his eyes. "I don't want to do that."

"Gwen doesn't know what to believe. You've betrayed her trust."

"Tell her—"

"Wood!" Mamey grabbed him. "Tell her yourself."

They were standing in his front room.

"I wouldn't—"

"You wouldn't what?"

"I wouldn't know what to say."

"If it's over, you have to tell her." Mamey looked glum. "Is there some other woman?"

Wood shook his head, then his trunk twisted, like an insect trying to wriggle out of its skin. "It's not that." Mamey, he knew, had her own ideas about Papaya, and they were foolishly naive. "I don't understand what's happening to me. The things I'm doing, the emotions I'm— I can't explain."

"She's in love with you. She thought you felt that way about her."

"I did. I still do."

"Well, why won't you speak to her?"

"It's hopeless. I'm not what she wants."

"What makes you think that?"

"Gwen wouldn't stay with me. I'm a writer without a future."

"You're working on—"

"I'll be penniless in a few months," he said.

"Is it really about money?" Mamey was surprised.

"She's like you. She wants children. A family."

"People figure these things out."

"I'm imagining something else."

Mamey studied him. As the seconds passed, her gaze softened. She took his hand. "What are you imagining?"

Wood swallowed. "The magic is gone. There's only wanting and not having. I couldn't bear that."

She sighed. Then she nodded. "Let's go for a walk. There's someone I want you to meet."

The walk took them down Margaret Street. The foot traffic was thin, and people were clothed in casual wear. It was as if the Fest had never occurred. The declining sun was behind Mamey, and the rosy glow shone through her hair, striating her cheek.

As they reached the Truman intersection, Wood could see the front of the church.

"Jesus?" He shook his head. "I know you mean well, but he's not for me."

"We're not here for Jesus," she said.

They continued past the church doors. Above, twin steeples rose into the sky, each with a cross at its top. Mamey left the pavement, taking a walkway that led beside the church's west wall, between small palms and across a clipped lawn. Wood followed.

At the end of the walkway was a wall of rock, thirty feet high. In a niche near the top, Wood saw a pale statue. A woman with a cloth on her head held her hands before her in prayer.

"Who is it?" he asked.

"Our Mother," Mamey said.

Wood regarded the stony face. Her eyes were open, but her lips were sealed.

"She appears in times of need," Mamey said. "I've been asking her to—"

"What?"

"Help you."

As if on cue, the church bells began to ring.

Wood turned and gazed at the steeples towering over them. They were unnaturally sharp, like Papaya's breasts. The church, it seemed, was a giant sculpture of her, lying on her back. Mamey was facing her icon of worship, and so was he. They stood there in silence till the tolling ended.

"I'm at the Hotel Tramposo," Papaya said. "The room has a giant bed. I'm here, stretched out on it, wishing you were beside me."

"I can't put you out of my mind, for even a second."

"When is your flight?"

"Tomorrow afternoon."

"No costumes," she said. "No craziness. Just Wood and Papaya."

"Where should I stay?"

"What a question," she said. "You're staying with me."

Wood was to meet her at a club, Sala de Cine, at 6 p.m. His plane landed at the Havana airport on schedule. He shouldered his backpack, made it through immigration, exchanged some dollars for pesos and found a taxi.

On the way into town, he got his first look at Cuba

through the glass. The roads were torn up and the buildings decaying; moving crowds flanked the highway, on foot and shabbily dressed. A good lesson, he thought, for someone starting love fresh. Life was uncertain, but no one was fussing.

As the sun set, the cab pulled up in front of Sala de Cine. Wood grabbed his backpack and stepped out.

The club was upscale and offbeat. There was a bar near the entrance, and on the wall to the right, behind the diners, a silent film was projected while a pianist played along. As Wood took a seat at the bar, the theme went minor and an armless Lon Chaney appeared.

Wood ordered a neat martini. At 6:20, he ordered a second, and at 6:45 a third. At 7:30, through the club's glass facade, he saw a white and plum Fairlane convertible pull up. The driver opened the passenger door and Papaya stepped out. She was dressed in white—a skintight lamé top and tights, with a flaring cloak.

As she entered, heads turned. She opened her arms and greeted him loudly. He rose to embrace her and they stood at the bar while she laughed and talked about the places she'd been and the sights she'd seen. He teased her about calling attention to herself. She teased him back, fingering the metal collar tips on his black satin shirt, while Chaney, heart-struck, made pitiful faces behind her.

Papaya lifted Wood's drink and downed what remained of it. Her polished claws clicked on the martini stem. "Let's see what's out back," she said.

At the rear was a patio open to the night. Couples were

smooching to a live bass and a slow trombone. Papaya hooked his arm, pulled him close and rubbed her thigh against his. "Let's go somewhere else."

Wood grabbed his backpack from the bar and put it in the Fairlane. Papaya gave the driver orders. The man tipped his straw fedora and off they went.

Papaya's profile was magnetic, her breasts more pointed than ever. Beneath her top, Wood imagined a bullet bra. If you were too close, she could put your eye out.

"What are you looking at?"

"Extra bait on the hook," he said.

"We're all married to our mirrors, conscious or not. I'm just more self-aware. I know what I'm doing."

Their destination was on a residential street in Miramar. The club was packed with overdressed kids dancing to a Cuban emo band. Papaya couldn't stand it. The next stop was a night spot in Central Havana with a novelty act—an overweight singer who wore funny hats. They were led to a table and Wood ordered drinks. The crowd found humor in the goofy show, but Papaya did not. As the waitress appeared with their drinks, she rose to leave. Next was a restaurant where dancers performed under purple light, whirling and leaping among the diners. Papaya was particular about seating and created a disturbance. A few minutes later she stood, flared her cloak and strode through the dancers, headed for the exit. Wood hurried after her. Outside, she gave the driver fresh orders.

"Slow down," Wood laughed.

She looked out the window. "I need to have some fun."

The Fairlane pulled up beside a horde of valets and doormen. Papaya traipsed past them without saying a word. They climbed a winding stair to the roof of a derelict factory. Amid tables where people sat and drank, an old brick smokestack towered into the sky. "You can climb it," the waiter said when he brought their drinks.

Wood followed Papaya across a catwalk and up a ladder that rose into the smokestack's blackened interior.

She turned her face up and screamed. "I want you," he boomed. As their voices echoed in the stack, she kissed him and put her hand on his groin. "Too long" she sighed, spilling her drink on his shirt. Wood let go of his, and it shattered on the stones below. He put his hands on her breasts.

"Not here, not yet," she said, slipping from his grasp.

The next stop was a club with a Soviet theme, where the waitresses wore Red Army uniforms. And the one after that was outdoors, at the water's edge, with a live salsa band. Papaya climbed onto the concrete seawall. Wood followed, and they stood there together, watching the waves pound below. She began to dance, balancing on the capstone, moving her hips and lifting her arms like a flamenco doña, eyeing the crowd on one side and the crashing waves on the other.

"That's enough for one night," she said finally, lowering her arms. And they headed back to Central Havana.

In the Fairlane, Wood embraced her. Papaya's lips parted, her nostrils flared. He reached his hand behind her neck to draw her head closer, and his lips found hers. As the kiss drew out, her breath quickened. When she finally let go, he thought, she'd be something to behold. They were back in the dance that had started the night they met.

Then he felt her hand on his chest. She was pushing him away.

"Wait," she said.

Wait? For what? Her eyes were on the driver.

"Not in the car," she whispered.

"Pretend he's not there." Wood kissed her neck.

"No." She pushed with both hands now. Her nails dug in.

Wood gripped her waist.

"Let me go," she said.

He slid his hand between her thighs.

"I said no." There was fury in her voice.

Wood let go.

The Fairlane pulled up in front of the Tramposo. Papaya was shaking her head at him. "You've spoiled it."

You planned this, he thought.

"I want it as much as you do," she said.

He was speechless, quivering with rage.

"Tomorrow," she said.

What can I do to hurt you? he thought.

"Do you hate me?" she said.

"I hate myself for wasting my time with you."

She sighed. "Things will be different tomorrow. We'll spend the day together." Papaya touched his cheek. "Meet me in the lobby at nine, for breakfast."

"I thought I was staying here."

"You need to get control of yourself." Papaya opened the car door. "Hotel," she ordered the driver. She looked at Wood. "You'll find a room nearby."

She stood on the paving and closed the door. Then her back was to him. With her hair flowing over her shoulders and her cloak flapping, she swept past the doorman.

At nine the next morning, Wood handed his backpack to the Tramposo's bell captain. Papaya was in the lobby, waiting. She was in casual clothing, a white blouse and khaki pants.

He crossed the marble floor, on guard, emotions in check. She opened her arms, stepped forward and embraced him. She put her lips to his, and the kiss was warm.

"I'm sorry about last night," he said.

"I am too. You frightened me," she laughed.

She led the way up a coiling staircase bordered with potted palms. Music came from above, resonant, tragic, lushly romantic. In the breakfast room, two violinists were playing.

Papaya was relaxed and talkative. As they ate, she unfolded her past.

"I was an only child, a child of privilege, without many friends. My father doted on me, and my mother hated me for it." Her mouth was wry, but her eyes were soft.

"I was sent away. I attended boarding schools in New England and Europe. I felt alone and unwanted, and unattractive. I was twenty before I started to ripen." She took a deep breath, lowering her lids as her breasts rose. "My parents died in a boating accident. I was in Switzerland when it happened. I realized I no longer had a reason to think of America as my home."

Wood slid his hand across the table. She smiled and took it, then the air went out of her smile.

"In my last year of school, I fell in love with a wild man. I jumped out of airplanes with him. We trekked the Darién Gap. We dove the Azores and swam with devil rays. There was a peak in the Andes— He never came back."

A musical piece had ended, and the diners were applauding. Papaya did as well. After that, she skimmed over a sequence of dead-end affairs, hopes raised and dashed. Her blue eyes were calm and guileless.

Wood set his napkin aside. "What do you need from me? What can I do?"

"Forgive me if I'm less than the Papaya of legend."

"The woman I'm with this morning," he said, "I'd stay with forever."

"I want to show you the roof terrace," she said.

They rode the lift up. From the terrace, all of Havana was visible—the harbor, the palace of the fallen dictator, the cobbled streets and faded two-stories, the decaying villas, the abandoned factories, and a lone power station still belching smoke.

Papaya asked about his marriage, and why it had failed. "I didn't know who she was," Wood replied. He tried to explain, but the story was more confused than he liked. She could see him struggling and she clasped his hand. "Love is a puzzle," Papaya said.

They stood together, gazing in silence at the disordered world around them. The roof terrace, with its pool and cabana, was an island of fancy in a sea of chaos.

"Today let's walk," she said.

They exited the hotel, crossed the boulevard and strode through a park into Old Havana. The narrow streets were busy. There were Cubans and tourists, school kids and teachers, workers and shoppers. They followed the foot traffic down a long arcade. By the curb, a black man in a white shirt unloaded green bananas from a blue truck. Flower vendors surrounded by buckets of blooms were trimming and tying.

Wood was talking and Papaya was laughing. A water truck made the rounds, pumping deliveries to homes and shops through a large hose. She grabbed his arm and pointed. A woman in a second-story apartment shouted to a man below and lowered a bag on a rope. The man removed coins, placed peppers, cucumbers and carrots in the bag, and the woman hoisted her purchase. Wood peered into Papaya's eyes. The gab, the buoyancy— They were finally in tune.

The sun, the markets, the cars from the fifties— Old Havana was like a memory of happier times. Wood remembered how things had been when he first met Vadette. Papaya was beautiful, authentic, with a freedom that filled the air around her.

Beneath a terracotta eave, a woman was seated amid

stacks of cages. Wood stooped, Papaya craned, admiring the miniature parrots and finches.

"That's what you'd do with me, if I let you," she said.

He nodded. "You'd have to beg for seed."

They passed a warehouse where meat was being butchered. "Can you take it?" she asked. Wood smiled and they stepped inside.

The space was dimly lit, dingy and reeking. Men in green vests stood behind counters, wielding knives and cleavers. One butchered loins, one livers; one butchered kidneys and hearts; still another cut ribs; and another, tongues and hooves. A man was prying flesh off a pig's head with a letter opener.

"Your old boyfriend," Wood said, eyeing the skull.

"He was good to me," Papaya sighed. She linked her arm through his.

After lunch, they walked around the Plaza and down a side street lined with shops. One caught Wood's eye. Through the window, it looked like a monarch's stateroom, with dark Victorian furniture and a checkered floor.

He opened the door and they entered together.

"What do you do here?" he asked.

"We make perfumes," a short spectacled woman replied.

"Can you make one for her?"

"Sí, sí, of course. You choose the scents. Who will decide?"

Wood looked at Papaya. "We'll do it together."

Papaya laughed.

The woman collected the fee from Wood and took her

seat behind an elevated bench surrounded by beakers, vials and hundreds of small bottles, arranged in tiers.

She selected a few, removed the stoppers and waved them under their noses.

"Too delicate," Wood said.

"Too sweet," Papaya winced.

"I like this one," he nodded.

"It's not me," she said.

"You are happy," the woman asked her, "or serious?"

"Serious," Wood answered.

"Happy I'm with him," Papaya said. "But serious, yes."

Another bottle passed under his nose. "This is part of her," Wood said. "Her strength, her boldness."

Papaya sniffed. "Yes, that's me."

The woman set the bottle aside. She tried a number of other scents on them without success. And then:

"This one," Wood said.

Papaya sampled the fragrance.

"It's supernal," he said. "Unearthly."

Her eyes met his.

"Does the bold one go with it?" Wood asked.

"Very well, I think," the woman replied.

"There must be a gnawing note," he said. "Something subversive."

Papaya's lips parted, as if she was going to protest.

"How about this?" The woman unstoppered a bottle and raised it between them. "It's an aphrodisiac too."

"Perfect," Wood said.

Papaya hooked his belt with her finger and drew him close. He circled her waist and put his lips to hers.

When the kiss ended, Wood faced the woman. "I think we're done."

She put a beaker on a scale, used a pipette to add the oils, then mixed them on a rotating table with alcohol and poured the contents into a bottle.

Before she handed the bottle over, the woman took a stick with a cotton swab, dipped it in the perfume and passed it to Papaya.

"I want to smell good to you." Papaya dabbed the scent behind her ear.

"You smelled good to me in the slaughterhouse," Wood said.

By sunset, the crowds had thinned. Papaya checked a note in her hand and pointed toward the courtyard of a small hotel. They climbed a stairway and entered a paneled room with chestnut cabinets. The proprietor looked up from behind the counter.

"A torpedo," Papaya told him. "*Para mi hombre.*"

The proprietor motioned them into the adjoining room. There was a bar, and to one side a small desk with an old woman seated at it.

Papaya smiled at Wood. "Let's watch." And to the proprietor, "Rum for us both."

The old woman gathered loose tobacco in one hand, compressing the scraps with her fist, tearing pieces with her other hand to add to the bundle. She laid a leaf flat on the desk and rolled the scraps into it, tucking with her fingers, shaping with her palms.

"Firm but spongy," Papaya murmured in Wood's ear.

The woman moistened her fingers and turned the ends between them.

"I'll get it started," Papaya said, and the old woman handed the cigar to her. She motioned to Wood, and they sat at the bar.

The proprietor raised a dry sprig and lit its leaves. When they were fiery, Papaya turned the cigar's tip in the flame and drew on it. Smoke crept from between her lips, swirling and ivory. "It's ready for you," she said, and she passed the cigar to him.

Wood put it between his teeth, closed his mouth around it and drew. The taste was musky, the texture gummy. Papaya raised the rum to her lips. When she lowered it, Wood kissed her. Their tongues crawled over each other, sharing the liquor and smoke.

"Know what I'm thinking about?" she said.

Wood shook his head.

"Yes you do. We've both been thinking about it all day."

After settling with the proprietor, they took a taxi back to the Tramposo.

They entered the lobby together, arm in arm.

Wood followed Papaya to the elevator. A man in a suit, with an earpiece, was standing there, watching people come and go. He studied Papaya. As the man's attention turned to Wood, Papaya let go of his arm.

When they exited the elevator, she moved down the hall with a determined stride. Wood hurried to keep up. As her steps slowed, he drew beside her. Papaya looked intent, her brow smooth, her lips set.

She stopped before a door and stared at it. The silence stretched out.

"Are we going in?" Wood said.

Papaya didn't reply. She reached into her pant pocket and pulled out her key.

"Is something wrong?" he asked.

"I'm a difficult woman." She faced him.

Wood laughed. "Tell me something I don't know."

"I'm not what you think." Her gaze was distant, as if she was looking through him. "When I fall, I fall hard."

There was fear in her eyes. The ice was gone. They were limpid pools.

"I'll be helpless. Weak. Not the Papaya you know."

He nodded, trying to reassure her, wondering what she meant.

An odd smile, bitter, ironic. Papaya lowered her chin.

"I'm not going to do this," she said, raising her room key.

He watched her, uncomprehending.

She leaned toward him to kiss him. She was saying good-night.

"What is this?" he protested.

Papaya shook her head.

"You're out of your mind." He grabbed her shoulders. "Open the door."

"Don't threaten me," she said. "You saw how far that got you last night."

"Papaya—" His tone was pained, conciliatory.

"No," she said angrily, wrenching free, fitting the key in the lock.

Wood put his hands on her rear.

"Bastard," she hissed, struggling with the door.

He tore at her hip, reaching to feel between her legs.

Papaya faced him, cheeks hollow, poison in her eyes. "I hate you."

Wood tugged at her waistband and thrust his hand down it. She turned, drove her elbow into his belly, clawed at the door handle, crossed the threshold and slammed the door in his face. "You baboon," she shrieked, "you freak!"

"You're sick," he stormed, sucking for breath. "Open the door!" He banged with both fists. "Open the fucking door!" He threw himself at it, kicking and pounding the insensible wood.

"You'll see me at your funeral," she crowed. "Wearing a party hat."

Someone was in the hall. Wood turned to find a room

service attendant a few yards away—a teenage boy with a tray on his shoulder, wavering, wide-eyed.

Wood swore and stamped past him. At the end of the hall, he stepped into the elevator and slapped the buttons. When it reached the ground floor, he hurried past the intelligence agent and crossed the lobby. A taxi was parked outside the double doors.

"To the airport," he told the driver.

Wood checked his ticket and collapsed in the aisle seat.

A small woman with a pale face was beside him, reading a book with a Spanish title.

"You look lonely as hell," he muttered.

"I look like I feel," she said, putting the book down.

"Sorry. You're an American."

She nodded. "I'm on Key West now."

Her hair was short and sandy, and she had a purple birthmark below her ear. She turned her cheek. His comment had hurt her. "What's your name?"

"Annona," she said.

"I'm Wood. If it helps, I'm worse off than you."

"How do you know?"

"I know," he said.

The airliner was backing away from the gate. As it taxied toward the runway, Annona asked what he was doing in Havana. Wood told her about Papaya. And then, as the jets roared and the plane rose into the night sky, he told her about Gwen and his time in Key West, and the breakup with Vadette in San Diego.

"It wasn't like that for me," Annona said. "I have a child. The divorce was just made final."

"Your ex-husband's in Florida?"

She shook her head. "He's in Cuba. He's a civil engineer. Swedish. He's working on the port at Mariel. He's going to stay."

"And you?"

"I'm not sure what Kjell and I will do. The Key is close to his father, but America's not his home. Neither is Cuba. He was born in Sweden. That's where we lived until two years ago."

"Where are you from?"

"Cudjoe Key," she said. "I'm an island girl. I just found a job. I'm a receptionist at a guesthouse near South Beach."

"What happened—"

"He got tired of me," she said. "He's with someone else."

"He's a fool."

"You were right," she said. "I *am* lonely as hell. If you need a—"

"I appreciate the offer."

"Please don't think—" She turned away. "I'm not ready for that."

Annona's home was on Tropical. Her husband wanted Kjell and her in a nice place, she said. Her car was at the airport, so she offered him a ride to Old Town. Then, when she learned he hadn't eaten, she insisted on taking him home with her. As they approached, a storm broke.

The house was modern, with a high stucco wall and a wrought iron gate. Annona parked the car in the drive and led him through the rain, along a flagstone path, toward the front entry. As she unlocked the door, she put her forefinger over her lips. They stepped quietly into the living room.

"Let me see if he's settled," Annona whispered, motioning Wood toward the couch. Then she disappeared down the hall.

Wood circled the room. There were potted plants and a piano. On a buffet stood a framed photo of Annona and a man with his arm around her. A boy was seated between them. He might have been seven or eight when the photo was taken.

Annona returned with an older woman, and the two talked about Kjell. Then the older woman stepped into a room off the entry and closed the door.

"Our live-in," Annona said. "It's alright." She took a plate of fruit and cheese from the fridge and motioned. "We can sit in the cabana."

Wood followed her across the patio and around the pool. The cabana was at the far end with a lounge bed beneath it.

The walls behind were matted with bougainvillea, and a small tree was planted to one side. He sat on the lounge bed. She put the plate on a small table and lowered herself beside him with two feet of space between.

What was it? he wondered. Her charm was muted, and his snubbed lust had faded; but something about her drew him powerfully. Without a word, as if she had heard his thoughts, Annona edged closer. Their eyes met, then she put her arm through his, rested her head on his shoulder and squeezed against him. It was sorrow, he thought.

Without Papaya, without Gwen— That was all he had left.

He kissed her forehead. She didn't respond. What was she thinking? She seemed to be waiting.

He kissed her lips. She put her hand on his knee, but her agitation was palpable. It would be hard for her, Wood thought, with her son, here in their home.

He turned her face up. She closed her eyes, and he kissed her again. His fingers found the catch at the back of her dress and unfastened it.

"Wood—" She sounded distressed. "I can't give you love. I'm in too much pain."

Her lips were trembling. Wood kissed them again. To his surprise, he was aroused. He caressed her thighs and Annona whimpered.

The rain fell harder. They were sheltered by the cabana roof, but all around them water was pouring.

Wood put his hand inside her dress and felt her breasts.

"What do you want?" she whispered.

She sounded helpless, vulnerable as a child.

Wood sighed and removed his hand. The desire he felt seemed perverse, and he was glad to cut it short. A thoughtless intimacy would do harm to them both.

He rose. It was less than a mile, and the rain would be warm. "I'm going to walk home," he said.

Without waiting for her response, he turned, circled the pool and recrossed the patio. When he reached the living room door, he opened it and stepped inside, pulling it behind him—slowly, stopping short of hearing the *click* of the latch. He stood there, confused, berating himself, feeling all at once like a coward without knowing why. Then, overcome by some unexplainable instinct, he turned, swung the door open again and retraced his steps.

Annona was on the lounge bed, bent over, her head in her hands.

He sat her up and removed her dress, gently but quickly. She did nothing to stop him. Wood lifted her and lay her on the lounge, then he stripped off his clothing and stretched out beside her.

At first, it seemed everything he did hurt her. Her skin was unnaturally soft, so tender in places that contact—even the meekest—pulled her apart. Her voice was a bleat, high-pitched and intermittent. And her heart wouldn't open. He could see it, green and lopsided, scaled with shining bosses—a varnish of tears that had fallen so thickly no one would ever gain entrance again.

But slowly, flaws were revealed and the hurts were bared. Wood felt her suffering in his belly, in his fingers, deep in his chest. She was mastering her fear, sharing the depth of her defeat, touching his with her own. He could feel their sorrows mingling.

As she'd warned, she had no love to give. But there was failure in abundance, and she gave that freely, a gut-wrenching failure that was all-consuming. Her injured heart opened. It wasn't amorphous. It was divided inside, sectioned into pockets soft as custard. Her sweetness was sour, cream-white and weepy, with an abject tang and a shivering submission that caught at the back of his throat.

His own failure welled up—that he was neither child nor man, husband nor lover; that fate had orphaned him and forced him to orphan himself; that he'd lived a dream of love all his life; that he'd abandoned a woman to shadow a demon; that trusting his instincts had delivered him here.

Remarkably, they reached a peak together. It was no revelation of bliss, but rather a convulsion of love once imagined, vital and nourishing, now dashed to myth, absurd and fanciful and lost forever.

When it was over, Annona stroked his hair and put her hand on his chest, trying to be grateful. But she wasn't able. She turned away and curled on her side. Wood thought of his mother, on the bed she would die in, barely able to speak or move. He rose, retrieved his clothes and pulled them on. Rain was no longer falling. The storm seemed to have ended. Wood crept through the house and out the front door.

As he started along Tropical he began to sob. He sobbed all the way down Flagler to William, and was still weeping when he turned onto South. He couldn't stop.

He crossed Elizabeth, heart pounding, hands shaking, and when he reached Simonton, he saw the familiar sign through his tears.

It was late, but Refugio was full. As he elbowed his way to the bar, Wood saw Auntie standing beside a young man, shaking her finger. When she spotted him, her expression changed. She made a beeline toward him, pushing bodies aside, alarm in her eyes.

"Wood, oh Wood. What's happened?"

He shook his head, unable to speak. Her concern was genuine.

"It's alright," Auntie assured him, circling his waist.

He caught his breath, wiping his tears. He was glad to see her.

"I've been with Papaya," he said.

Auntie's face drew close. Her hair was stringy and her brow rumpled. But she had a creamy scent. "Papaya," she said, "and every fruit on the Key but me."

She wore a low-cut blouse, and she pushed her oversize breasts against him. The deep cleavage mouthed, opening and closing like a fish out of water.

"Time for Coconut." She slid her hand into her dress and scooped a breast. "It's Auntie you need."

"What are you doing?"

"No one will notice," she said.

"That's not funny."

Auntie regarded him. Then she let go of her breast and grabbed his arm. "Come with me. Come on, come on."

Wood was too defeated to resist.

She led him across Duval, down a narrow street, into Bahama Village. The cottages were small, and many were in disrepair. She pointed at one.

"That's my place," she said. "It's not hard to find."

A big tree rose from the garden, the biggest on the block. Both the tree and the cottage were covered with vines, long fringes that fell from the eaves and branches.

As they passed through the gate, chickens scattered. "Foolish boy," she muttered. A homeless man sleeping beneath the tree rolled over. The porch was weathered and creaky. Auntie opened the warped door and led him across the threshold, into the dim interior.

She switched on a lamp. Around him were carved antiques, fine woods and rich fabrics, his surprised face in an oval mirror. "They buy me things," Auntie said.

How many men had she escorted here? She gripped his shoulders and turned him to face her, squaring his head, straightening his arms against his sides, repeating some practiced ritual. Then she unbuttoned his shirt and removed his pants, draping his clothing over the arm of an old wing chair. She examined herself in the mirror and primped her hair, and when she faced him again, she was undoing her dress. Her breasts were large and wrinkled.

"You're shameless," he said.

Auntie laughed.

He put his hand on one and pinched the nipple. A sound of approval rose in her throat. Then she clasped his wrist and led him toward the rear.

A narrow hall. A dim room. A brocade chair and a four-poster. The bed had a woven coverlet.

She eased him onto it, then she clambered over him, cooing encouraging words, dragging her nipples across his cheeks.

Wood froze. The tips were wet. There was milk leaking from them.

"For you." Auntie placed her palm beneath her breast and offered it to him.

He stared at the dripping stem.

"Take all you can," she said. "Don't be shy."

Wood turned away, repulsion mixed with his shock.

"I have to use the bathroom." He slid from beneath her and rose.

He crossed her bedroom and entered the hall. Through an open doorway, he spotted a toilet. He slipped through and turned on the light.

It looked like an herbalist's lab. On one side was a window box full of plants with handwritten labels—Goat's Rue, Brutebane, Silver Thistle. On the other, shelves were packed with cuttings, dried or soaking in bottles. On the counter were a clutter of pastes in marked jars. Wood stuck his finger in a white ointment and wrote *Help* on the mirror. Then he turned on the faucets full blast, slid through the doorway and hurried to the front of the house.

He pulled on his pants and shirt, opened the door, crossed the porch and started down the street barefooted. How long had Auntie been offering her milk to strangers? No wonder she was deranged. An old black man on the corner nodded to him, as if he'd seen the unweaned bachelors coming and going for years.

9

When Wood woke the next morning, he found a message from Callie on his phone. It might have been troubling under other circumstances, but the sound of her voice, and her raw emotion, buoyed his spirits.

"I can't pretend," she said. "It's plain talk now. No dressing it up. No scheme, no method—

"You're mine. You belong to me," she poured her heart out. "I'm woman enough. This sweet thing you're stuck on, she doesn't need you like I do. She'll find someone else. Please, Wood. Please, please, give us a chance."

Wood played the message again, feeling her warmth and devotion. "I love you too," he said on the third play. "You're more than I deserve. Much more."

He pulled on briefs and stepped into the bathroom to shave. But when he looked in the mirror, the shave was forgotten. He just stood there, trying to make sense of what had happened and who he'd become.

He retrieved his phone and called Piña.

When she answered, he said, "Can I see you?"

"Sure. I'm at home."

Wood drove to Stock Island, unsure what he'd say. Tray was too brainy, and he had a crisis of his own. Callie couldn't see past her need. Mamey didn't understand the depth of his problem. Piña— He had faith in her judgment.

He honked as he pulled up in front of the trailer.

The door flew open, and she greeted him with a hug.

"Laundry time," she said, kicking a pile of clothing aside.

Wood collapsed on the bed, and Piña sank beside him. He reached for her purse, opened it and pulled out her pipe. "Should we get high?"

She shrugged. "Should we?"

Wood considered the question, then put the pipe back.

"I've been thinking," he said. "About us."

"Oh yeah?"

"I love you, Greentop."

She could see his sadness.

"You're making me worried," she said.

"Do you want to get married?"

"Get outta here," Piña laughed. "You're with Gwen." She peered at him. "Aren't you?"

Wood shook his head. "I fucked it up."

"What did you do?"

"I went silent. I didn't see her. I didn't call or text. I didn't answer her messages. I just disappeared."

Piña waved his concern away. "I did that to Stubby. It didn't make any difference. He won't leave me alone."

"You had a reason."

"Maybe you did too," Piña said. "You still want her?"

He nodded. "But I've lost her. Pretty sure about that."

"She's still thinking about you, I bet."

"I was chasing Papaya," he said.

"You? I thought you were smarter than that."

"I can't tell Gwen."

"You have to be honest with her," Piña said.

"What will she think?"

"I know what I'd think. Papaya's bullshit. I'd want to know who you were really with. I'd want to hear that I was better than she was: smarter, funnier, sexier. I'd want to believe that you cared about me, and what happened would never happen again."

"That would do it?"

Piña was silent. "No," she said finally. "I'd want to know why."

Something crashed into the trailer, dishing them both to the floor.

"Stubby," Piña hissed, her eyes big as eggs.

As Wood rose, a handgun popped, and the sink window shattered.

"Get out," Piña shrieked.

Wood grabbed her hand and leaped for the door. He barreled into it, and the door screamed back on its hinges. As he dropped to the gravel, Wood saw a small man lurching toward him, hunched like an ape. He was burly and snarling, waving a snub-nosed revolver.

"Goddammit," Piña bellowed.

Wood straight-armed Stubby, sending him tumbling in the grass. Then he hurried Piña to his car. He got it started before Stubby regained his feet. The car lurched forward as another shot fired. Then a third and fourth as Wood made a sharp turn. The last shot spidered his rear windshield.

"We're going to the police station," Wood said as they sped away.

"Are you crazy?" Piña gasped.

"We'll go to my place. You're staying with me."

"Gwen will love that," she said. "Take me to Lychee's house. I'll deal with Stubby tomorrow."

No excuses, no delays. Gwen was at work, but that didn't matter. Wood sat at his kitchen table with the phone before him and made the call, reminding himself of the praying Mamey had done.

When Gwen answered, he invited her out.

She refused. "This has been hard for me," she said. "Don't make it harder."

"I just want you to listen. To understand what happened."

"I don't want to know," she said. "Please, don't call again."

And the line went dead.

It was every bit as bad as Wood feared. But he hewed to Piña's advice and plotted another course.

After work, Gwen often biked to a supermarket in New Town. She exited the market that evening with a bag in her arms and secured it in the basket. But when she went to free her bike from the rack, she groaned. Another rider had cabled his front wheel to hers. Then she recognized the bike and straightened, looking around.

Wood stepped from behind a parked car and hurried toward her. "My mistake," he said, as if he was a perfect stranger.

Gwen laughed despite herself, while he knelt and removed the cable.

"Thirty minutes," he begged her. "Please."

She refused at first, but in the end, she agreed. "Thirty minutes. No more."

There was a delicatessen a short walk from the market. Wood carried her groceries. They sat across from each other, and he ordered a pair of ice teas. Gwen looked different. Her hair was bound up—the long waves were invisible. And there was a darkness around her eyes.

"Times a-wasting," she said.

He took a breath. "I've never felt—with any woman—what I felt with you."

She looked down, maintaining her reserve and distance. The relationship had been reset. He was a stranger again, on uncertain ground.

"I didn't know what love was," he said. "I didn't think it could be so familiar, so real. That was foreign to me."

Gwen frowned. He was confusing her.

"A woman, a precious one. Children. A family. With everything depending on me." He struggled with his words. "I was frightened. Frightened and tempted."

She was listening, but she was trying to protect herself. And he wanted to lie to protect her. But he knew he couldn't.

"I imagined a different kind of love—obscure, unfamiliar, mysterious. I made a fool of myself." Wood took a breath. "Chasing Papaya."

Silence. Then Gwen sighed.

"The strange thing," he said, "the thing I can't explain because I don't understand it, was that you were still with me. Your thoughts, your affection, the love—so genuine, so innocently given. A knot was tied that has never come undone."

Enough, he thought. *Let her react.*

Gwen's hands slid from the table into her lap. She pursed her lips. Then she bowed her head. "I wish we had talked."

Wood couldn't imagine that. What would he have told her?

"I wish you'd said something," she muttered. "Anything." Gwen lifted her chin, and the green eyes met his. "The silence, knowing nothing, was very hard."

He was about to speak, but he stopped himself. *Listen*, he thought.

"You opened a wound," she said. "I was married. I loved the man. But the love wasn't returned, and I refused to see it. I can't let that happen again."

"You're angry," he said.

She nodded. "I am."

Angry, he thought, *and afraid*. He was asking a lot.

"I've lost your trust," he said.

She nodded, and a sound like a whimper escaped her.

That shook him—her weakness, her vulnerability. She was letting him see how much misery he'd caused her, and the sight so distressed him, it distorted her appearance. Her chin seemed too small, her eyes too large. Her lips were swollen and trembling.

"Forgive me," he said. "Please forgive me."

Her self-assurance was gone. Was there anything he could do to restore it? What had he done? With the guilt and regret came a realization of how lucky they'd been and how miserable his life was without her.

"I can't let you go," Wood said.

Piña was right. Gwen hadn't given up on him.

They sat in the deli for a couple of hours, and as they talked, the distortions in Gwen's appearance faded. Her composure returned, and so did her beauty.

"We found each other at a difficult time," he said. "I knew so little. I still have so much to learn. I wish I was farther along."

"Life isn't simple," she said, "for any of us."

"You and I— We were meant for each other," Wood said. "I believe that."

When they were walking to their bikes, he reached for her hand. "Can we ride back together?"

They spoke little on the way to her apartment, but when they arrived, he begged her to have dinner with him. Nothing fancy. Something quick at Dos Pesos. "We're talking," he said. "I don't want it to end."

Gwen's brows relaxed. There was sympathy in her emerald eyes.

Her confidence returned steadily. While they were eating, he could see her fighting her fears, trying to put doubt aside.

"It's a beautiful night," he said as they left the restaurant. "Would you walk to South Beach with me?"

She consented, and they strolled down Duval together.

When they reached the sand, they went barefoot, stepping out under the rustling palms and the blinking stars. At the water's edge, Wood faced her. He raised his hand slowly and touched her temple.

"You have such beautiful hair," he said. "Will you let it down?"

She removed the pins and unbound the braids. He helped her untwist them. Together, they combed their fingers through the dark locks.

"Gwen," he said. "Will you spend the night with me? At my place?"

She raised her brows. "Cozy."

"It can be a home too."

She looked past his shoulder. Then she sighed. "I still care for you."

"I love you, Gwen. More than anything."

When they reached his apartment, he stopped at the bottom of the stairs. He was eager to embrace her, but first he said things he believed she needed to hear.

"Whatever the future holds for me, I want you in it. You're the most important thing in my life, from here on."

Gwen smiled.

Wood kissed her cheek, and her smile grew until it was a bubble of joy around them. He circled her with his arms and they slid together, finding their private language again, sightless, wordless, trepidatious but acutely aware.

They spent the night in each other's arms, a night like none before. It owed nothing to the past. The doubts and fears required a new kind of courage. Was his handicap still with him? Was she making a mistake? Wood did nothing to protect himself. Gwen gave more than ever, every last sigh from her fathomless heart.

In the late hours, Wood lay beside her with his hand on her hip. "With you," he said, "I know why we all need love so badly."

She leaned her head on his shoulder. Her lips moved, and Wood heard "*Toujours*." The future she'd dreamed of— She was wishing it back.

Gwen turned to face him. "I never stopped hoping," she said. "While you were gone, a friend who reads cards showed me my future."

"Not Nan."

"You know her? She's so wise. My man is the Knight of Cups. He rides a white horse, bearing a gift for the one he loves. He's a romantic, and he trusts his heart. He will sweep the past away. That's what Nan said. He'll change everything."

Wood touched her chin with his finger. "That's me."

"Please don't hurt me." Her dark eyes met his. "I'm feeling foolish. And weak. I don't trust myself. I have so many flaws. I'll never be Papaya."

He regarded her, fearful, unsure what to say.

"What was she like?" Gwen asked.

Wood took a breath. "Cruel," he murmured. "Uncaring, unfeeling. I thought I was the exception, that I'd be the one to please her. I was wrong."

"Can you forget her?"

"There's nothing left in my heart but anger."

Gwen's lips were trembling. "Wood," she whispered.

He put his arms around her. "What's wrong?"

"When you vanished, I worried it was because I'd disappointed you in bed."

"That's not true."

"Papaya's way ahead of me, I know."

He laughed. "We didn't even—"

"I want to do things we haven't done before. I'm not afraid. Will you help me?"

"If we're going to explore," he said, "I'll need your help too."

They made love again, as tyros this time—self-conscious and fumbling, but eager to learn, forgiving of each other's mistakes.

The four walls of the room disappeared. Wood found himself on the island, the realm of love and growing things. He was in a wild orchard with a view of the sea, a lush place littered with fruit—loving gifts from generous hearts—and playthings from a carefree boy's youth. But the sweet treats were unsampled. The toys were unused. The slingshot lay where the boy had left it, along with his coins and a folding knife.

He was older now. And the woman he loved—so was she.

Below a large tree, Gwen stood open and ready, ripe and fragrant—sectors bulbed, her kaleidoscope flesh glittering with prismatic hues. She was the island's glory, its most precious fruit. And he was its hero, sure and full-hearted, returning home.

The next day, they walked the White Street Pier. When they reached its end, Gwen swept into his arms, vibrant and unreserved, all her jets burning as if they had never turned off. They kissed and kissed, and she cried and cried.

For two weeks, they spent every free hour together. When Gwen was at work, Wood wrote in his log, trying to track what was happening. Gwen was human, she had her flaws. And of course he had his. They were talking about their differences now, and as their awareness grew, a new ease emerged. From their words and actions, a language was born—the language of a couple.

Wood had a duplicate key made for his apartment, and on their return from a beach walk one evening, he presented it to her. She put it on her key ring, and when they reached his place, she did the honors.

"It's Saturday," Gwen said. "I want to go to Higgs Beach. There's something I'd like to show you."

They strolled down Reynolds Street till they reached the shore, then they walked to the surf line and followed it east. The sky was blue and the sand was warm. Gwen's smile was subtle, a sign of her hopefulness, being so understated.

The beach circled a large fenced-in area crowded with shrubs and trees. She led him to a shadowed entrance lined with palms and hung with vines. In a bricked arcade, an elderly man sat behind a desk. When he saw Gwen, he nodded. "Welcome," he said, lifting his chin, examining Wood through his spectacles.

Gwen led the way into a landscaped maze, shrubs and hedges, bridges and terraces, passing a spring where water flowed out of the rock, and another where an almond tree faced the sea. Beneath a gazebo, a man stood with a violin, playing three long notes—high, lower and higher still. Palm trees swayed above, green fingers waving. A threshold, Wood thought. The entrance to a meaningful life.

From the gazebo, a stone path led down. They reached a terrace bordered by orchids and roofed by a trellis.

"I came here," Gwen said, "when you didn't call."

They crossed the terrace, and the trellis striped them with sun. A path wound by a nursery and passed through an arch in the trunk of a giant tree. The arch was flanked by rooting branches sent down from above.

"It's a ficus," she said, taking his hand. "You walk through it together."

Beyond the arch was a small courtyard, where a man was sweeping leaves from the bricks. Gwen walked to a stone bench and sat down. Wood sat beside her.

"I'd sit on this bench and think about us."

The giant tree towered into the sky, thirty feet wide.

Gwen gazed at the courtyard. "It's a beautiful spot."

"Beautiful," he agreed.

She closed her eyes. "People get married here."

The three notes of the violin reached them on the breeze.

Wood met Tray for breakfast in Bahama Village. They sat outdoors, beneath a canvas umbrella, with hens and chicks bobbing around their feet. Six feet away was a small graveyard where markers memorialized fallen roosters.

"You look great," Tray said.

"You do too. How are things with Bijou?"

"Better. I'm going to propose."

Wood made his eyes wide. "Commitment."

Tray sighed. "By not saying 'yes,' I was just protecting myself."

"Against your own harsh judgment," Wood guessed.

The therapist nodded.

"Bijou's faith is a true one," Wood said. "You're as good as she thinks."

Tray's eyes laughed, still the skeptic.

"You see things others can't see," Wood said. "You help people, Tray. You've helped me."

"Have I?"

Wood nodded. "You've been right about so many things."

He explained what had happened in Cuba, then he told

Tray the story of his strange encounter with Annona the night he returned.

Tray raised his brows at the latter.

"I'm with Gwen now," Wood said. "She took me back."

"That's so good to hear," Tray smiled. "Come with me. I'm buying the ring tomorrow."

"You'll be a great dad."

Tray laughed. "When I look in the mirror, that's not what I see."

"I know," Wood sighed, scanning the menu. "What're you having?"

"Eggs, what else."

That afternoon, while Gwen was at work, a courier arrived at Wood's apartment with a handful of silver helium balloons and a box of Havana cigars. There was no note, and the sender was unidentified.

Wood punctured the balloons and carried them to the garbage, along with the Havanas. Then he wrote Papaya a text message. He told her how exciting she was to be with, how much he enjoyed her spontaneity, how stirred he was by her depth of feeling. But he thought it best if they didn't see each other again. "The hot and cold treatment was just too much."

That night, Gwen returned from work distraught. Raina,

her sister had called from Pompano Beach. Raina's daughter had fractured her arm. She was only eleven, and the break wasn't healing. They had to do surgery. Wood did his best to comfort Gwen, cooked a light dinner and put her to bed.

It was blistering hot. The sun was like a giant squeezed fruit, juices dripping from eaves, pulsing down the streets. The jewelry store was between a t-shirt shop and a bingo parlor.

Tray stooped over a glass display case, turning a ring with a champagne diamond between his fingers. "She'll like it." He looked at Wood.

"That's the one," Wood agreed.

"If there's a problem, come back and bring her with you," the woman behind the display case said. She had a hooked nose and dandruff.

"Don't I know you?" Wood said.

"Cashew." The woman extended her hand.

Wood shook it. "I want one too."

Tray regarded him, half amused.

"If you can do it," Wood said, "so can I. We'll get married together."

"You're serious."

Wood nodded. "Maybe I am." He looked at Cashew and pointed at the glass. "That's a nice pair."

The ring was silver, with a square cut diamond, and there was an engagement ring with it—a quarter-inch band with an inlay of green opal.

Cashew lifted them out. "For a special woman," she smiled.

On the way back from the jeweler, Wood got a text from Papaya. "Important," it said. "Have to talk. Call me as soon as you read this." Wood deleted the message.

At 3 p.m., she sent him another text. "Don't do this to me."

A half hour later, Papaya phoned. "I know you're listening to this," she said. "Please call. Please."

At 5 p.m., just before Gwen returned from work, Papaya left another voice message. "Can't you understand? I've chosen you. Don't freeze me out. Damn you, damn you! How can you be so cruel?"

"Is something wrong?" Gwen asked as they finished dinner.

Wood shook his head. "Thinking about Raina. How are they doing?"

"She wants me to come," Gwen said. "I can take a few days off. I think I should. You'll be alright—"

"Of course," he said. "Don't worry about me."

After dinner, Gwen put some clothes and toiletries in a

valise. They went to sleep in a frontal embrace and hugged each other most of the night. Then, some time before dawn, half-awake, Wood turned away. He faced the darkened window, feeling the gap, and when he dropped back to sleep, he found himself in a strange dream.

He dreamt he was speaking to Vadette from a great distance. The night carried his thoughts to her, like telepathy or prayer. He was recanting. He was sorry he had never understood her, sorry she had sought love with another man, sorry he had moved to the Key and thrown himself at so many women. And sorry—so sorry—he had met Gwen.

It's you I want, he said. Vadette was listening. She heard him. And then she was there, standing beside the bed. Wood rose and faced her. They were together again, and his future was in her hands. In return for his pledge of renewed love, she would reveal a secret—something she'd kept hidden all the years of their marriage. The wig fell to the floor and she freed her white hair. She unbound her corset, and pointed breasts pushed out. She straightened her knees and stiffened her back, gaining three inches. Then she peeled off her face. It was Papaya he'd married. She'd been his wife all along.

"Are you sure you're alright?" Gwen finished dressing.

"I'm just fine." He kissed her.

The morning sun rayed through the parted curtains.

"Maybe I should—"

"You promised them," Wood said. "They're expecting you. Don't worry."

"Call me in the car. I don't like leaving directly from work."

"I'll call. Drive carefully. Don't get distracted."

Ten minutes after Gwen left, he got a text from Papaya.

"It's true," she said. "Hot and cold. On and off. Wood, please. It's fear. I'm mad about you, but I'm afraid. I'm in love. I want to have sex with you, crazy sex, again and again. One more chance. Will you give me that?"

Wood circled the room with his phone in his hand. He opened the front door and stepped onto the porch, peering up and down the block, as if he expected to see her parked nearby.

He raised his phone, started to key in a reply, then deleted it and started again.

What was he doing? The badgering would end, sooner or later. He shook his head. The famous Papaya.

As he stepped back inside, his phone rang.

"Wood?"

"Um-hmm."

"I'm in Montevideo," she said. "But I'll be there Sunday. I can't talk now— I'll call tomorrow. Keep your phone with you. Everything's changed. Everything."

She hung up.

Wood laughed and shook his head.

After dinner, he reached Gwen. She was south of Vero

Beach. They had barely said hello when the signal dropped. He tried her again, but he couldn't get through. The next morning, she called first thing. It was a good thing she'd come, she said. Her niece was alright, but Raina was a wreck. Surgery was scheduled for early the following morning.

Wood worked on his log, and when lunch rolled around, he biked to Hao Zhidao. Guava was off duty and some chatty teens were seated at his table, so he ordered Twice-Cooked Pork to go. He biked back to his apartment and ate while he wrote. He'd just finished the carton when his phone rang.

Papaya again.

"What's up?" he said.

"I'm headed for Miami. Sunday's our day. If you have plans, cancel them."

"My last message was 'goodbye.'"

"You're angry with me. You wanted more in Havana."

"The answer is 'no.' Cry a little," Wood said. "Pretend you're sad."

"I don't have to pretend," she whimpered. "I am sad. Terribly sad. I should have given you what you wanted. I wanted it too. If you only knew— It's been lies till now. Lies, lies— I swear, I'm going to tell you the truth. I'm not the monster you think I am. You'll forgive me." She laughed. "There are a few things I know how to do."

Wood was silent. He remembered the cigar store in Havana. And that sweltering night, when Papaya lay twisting beside him, beaded with sweat.

"You missed me," she said.

"I forgot about you."

"Meet me part way," she said.

"Part way?"

"Marathon. There's a skipper I know. He can land us on a key of our own. No one else in the world. Just the two of us."

"Like Adam and Eve," Wood said.

"Naked in Eden. We'll start over. Together."

It was time to hang up, Wood thought. He reached for the empty bag and fished inside it. There was a fortune cookie at the bottom.

"I'm cutting all my ties," Papaya said. "I should have done that the night we met. Are you listening?"

"I'm listening." He removed the cellophane from the cookie.

"You're my lifeline now," Papaya said.

He cracked open the cookie. YOU ARE ABOUT TO GET WHAT YOU WANT, the fortune read.

"You'll have to be strong," Papaya warned.

Wood stared at the strip of paper.

"I'm letting go of everything else," she said.

He was silent, motionless.

"That's how Papaya is," she said, "with the man she loves."

She had the phone against her lips. Wood could hear her breath.

He set the fortune down.

"You're still crazy about me," she said. "Aren't you."

"Crazy," he said.

In the car, crossing the Keys, Wood was in a strange state. His mind was churning with visions of Papaya, but it was hatred he felt, not ardor. He would just as soon kill her as have sex with her. At the back of his mind, his misgivings about breaking faith with Gwen ticked like a bomb.

It was an hour to Marathon. He crossed the last bridge and made his way to the small harbor where the boat was docked.

She was waiting by the gangway, smiling as if she knew something he didn't. She was wearing a tank top and shorts, and looked breezy and relaxed, like that morning in Old Havana.

As he approached, she straightened, eyeing him directly. Did she expect an embrace?

Wood halted four feet away. He met her gaze, then he laughed. "Eau de Papaya."

"My favorite scent." Her smile was an innocent smile, but her lips twitched and her eyes darted. Her nails were chewed to the quick.

He looked around. "Quiet spot." The slips were full, the docks empty.

Papaya waved her hand. "I'm done with the Keys." She took a step toward him. "I want you to come with me."

"Where to?"

"Isla Grande. Chile— Tierra del Fuego. We'll stand on

the highest mountain at the end of the earth." She opened her arms and closed the distance, embracing him.

Wood felt her warmth and the points of her breasts.

"No boundaries," she said. "And no secrets. I mean it. No holding back."

She led him down the gangway, onto the boat, thighs gliding, hips shifting enticingly, controlled by hidden cogs. The skipper was tight-lipped, more accustomed to fishermen than lovers. He had packed snorkel gear and a lunch for them. As the two changed into swimwear, he fired up the engine and signaled to a dockhand to unmoor the boat.

They were leaving the slip when Papaya, now suited up, moved to the rail. She saw the dockhand, and he saw her.

"Babe," the man shouted.

Papaya quivered and looked away.

Wood stared. "Babe?"

She acted mystified. "He's a stranger to me."

As they left the harbor, an osprey perched on a harbor light looked down at them. Wood stood at the rail with Papaya beside him, watching the foam streaming back from the prow, feeling the shocks as the boat cut the swells. Neither spoke.

They motored for twenty minutes, then the skipper nodded to Papaya, and she and Wood put on the snorkel gear. "That's your paradise," he said as the island came into view. It was a small mangrove reef aproned with sand.

"I'll put your lunch there." He pointed at a knob of rock.

They moved to the stern, and at the skipper's word, they

dropped into the water together. Then the boat sped away.

The sea was turquoise and sinuous. When Wood looked, Papaya was sliding through the water beside him. She reached for his hand. He watched it waver in the current, then he kicked his fins, sending himself forward, not knowing or caring if she would keep up. She remained beside him, moving as he did, her shoulder touching, her thigh brushing his.

Were they in harmony again? Papaya's movements were graceful and self-assured. Her supple limbs, the curve of her hips, her wonderful breasts— There was no denying, she was a beautiful woman. The sea made her soft and human.

They drifted past ledges of rock, coral fans, angelfish, butterflies and yellow grunts. Papaya left his side and circled a trumpetfish. When she came back around, he felt for her waist. She shook him off and swam toward the surf. Wood followed. As they entered the shallows, he removed his fins and mask. She did the same, and they rose together, finding their footing in the pale sand.

"Stay here," she said, taking the gear from him. She hurried out of the water, dumped the stuff on the shore and waded back in.

"I want to be naked," she said when she reached him.

What are you doing? Wood thought. *You're in love with Gwen. You're going to marry her.*

Papaya closed her eyes and put her hands on his chest.

"Be gentle with me," she whispered. "I'm not what you think."

Wood put his lips to hers.

"What they say about me," she murmured.

He loosened her top, and her breasts came free. He touched one with a dripping finger.

"What they say," she whispered.

He untied her bottom and put his palm on her waist. She felt for his trunks and pulled them off. Then she pressed her naked body to his.

They sank together in the skim of surf. Papaya turned on her hip, then she lay on her back with the water lacing beneath her.

"I'm helpless," she said, gazing up at him. "If you want me, take me." And she lifted her arms.

After all her craft and deceit, was the way finally open?

Papaya closed her eyes.

Wood ran his fingers up her thigh, a native caressing his idol of worship after centuries of taboo. He put his hands in the sand by her shoulders and lowered himself, heart hammering. Had the time really arrived? Would a curse fall at the last moment?

The hissing froth bubbled over them. Papaya turned her cheek. Wood steeled himself. He felt his chest throbbing against her breasts. The fruit's skin parted, and he ventured inside.

The first taste took him aback. It wasn't creamy or sweet, canny or coy; it was dark and bitter, reticent, repelling. Papaya made his tongue flinch as if she'd been pickled, or had fermented, being hidden so long. Where was her sunshine, her richness, her yearning?

He expected a wondrous bounty, but he tasted only wariness and depletion. Was this all Papaya had to share? *She's holding back*, he thought. More lies, more cunning— His suspicions ran wild.

"I'm sorry," she said.

Wood stared at the face before him, disbelieving.

"Please," she said.

"You're not doing this."

"Accept me for what I am," she implored him. "I'm not Papaya."

"No? Who are you?"

"A fruit, special in my way. Melony," she whispered. "Bitter Melon."

Wood drew back.

"I couldn't help myself," she said.

He was speechless. What was she telling him?

"I fell for you," she said, "when you first arrived on the Key. You were looking for Papaya. So I pretended to be her."

Wood stared at the woman who'd haunted his dreams.

She took a breath. "I never intended to draw things out. I was going to come clean. But every time—" A tear fell from her eye. "I feared what would happen, once you found out."

Her boldness, her guile—

"I'm yours, if you want me," Melony said, inclining her hips. "I have no sweetness, but my taste is complex. I intrigue the senses, I perplex the mind. I linger on the tongue—"

The flesh she was offering was caustic and indigestible. It bristled with warts, it was choked with paste and seeds.

"Do you like it?" she asked. She was still smiling, but there was too much tooth showing.

As Wood watched, her smile dissolved.

"You're disgusted," she said.

For a moment, the blue eyes were limpid. Wood saw sufferance. Her lids lowered, as if she'd seen all she cared to at some earlier time. Then a laugh, curt and bleak—nothing remained of her deception other than to find some amusement in it.

"Get off me," she said, the blue pools icy again. "Get off, damn you!"

Wood lifted himself.

"You worm," she snarled, "You're all shriveled up."

A red fog clouded his vision, released from inside. He saw her face now behind a red screen. The blue eyes were gone, and the platinum hair—

"Look at you," she said. "Did Vadette cut them off?"

The air was red, and the water too. All he could see was red, and all he could feel was venom and seething.

"Did Vadette—"

The red inside him stained his chest. His front gleamed like chitin. Jointed red legs sprang from his sides. His arm bristled with twitching hairs. Papaya or Melony—whoever she was—seemed blind to the danger.

His first two fingers inflated and clacked. Scarlet pincers. They dove, parting and clashing to shear her head from her neck, missing by inches. Melony's head jerked from side to side, eyes white all around.

What are you doing? Wood thought. But the scorpion wasn't listening.

Her body hissed and clocked, flailing its arms, flexing its legs. His eight claws clinched her and the pincers dove, scissoring again. She convulsed. Choking sounds emerged from her throat as the tide washed over her. Her head was still attached to her neck, but the giant pincers were pushing it under.

Wood saw her terror through a veil of froth, her silver locks twisted around his chitinous wrist, a string of bubbles emerging from the corner of her mouth.

All at once, the red fog cleared.

The foam hissed away, the veil dissolved.

Melony's face was blue.

Wood grabbed her shoulders and lifted her from the flow. He circled her chest and dragged her onto dry sand. She pushed him away, rolling onto her side. She rose onto her knees and collapsed again, coughing and wheezing.

Numb but relieved, he was gasping as if he too had been underwater.

Melony shook her head like a dog, then she faced him, on all fours. Wood unhunched himself, wiping his mouth.

"A fantasy," he said between breaths. "That's what you gave me."

"That's what you wanted," she rasped.

All at once, Wood's vision drew back. It was as if Papaya—Melony—was a hundred miles away, and he was seeing her through a spyglass.

He retreated to the far end of the beach, and he remained there till the boat arrived to pick them up.

10

In his car, returning to Key West, Wood picked up two messages. The first was from Tray. "Bijou is thrilled," it said. The second was from Gwen. "Surgery went well. Raina's calm. I'm headed back. Love you." The message was two hours old.

Wood checked the cars in the lane beside him, glanced in the rearview mirror and stepped on the gas. His thoughts were confused, his judgment in ruin. Papaya, a delusion. Melony, bitter fruit. The taste she'd left wouldn't pass quickly. He hated her for playing on his fantasies, but it wasn't rage he felt now. It was guilt and remorse.

Why were his impulses so misguided? How could anyone trust him, if he couldn't trust himself?

With one hand on the wheel, he sent Gwen a text. "Dinner at Hao Zhidao at seven? Miss you."

The thought of being alone with himself in his apartment made him ill. He didn't dare record anything in his log. And the truth was too distressing to reflect on. If the scorpion had held Melony under a few moments longer—

"See you there," Gwen texted back.

When he arrived in Old Town, Wood parked his car on a side street near lower Duval. It was late afternoon and the crowds were gathering. He strode into a tourist club, found his way to the bar and began guzzling rum. When he left, it was dark outside and the neon was lit. The time was 7:20, and he was drunk.

He headed down the street, weaving through gawkers, barking at them to get out of his way. He stopped at a corner to listen to a starving musician and emptied his pockets into the fellow's hat. Then he began to sing along. Passersby were amused. A drink was handed to him to keep him fueled. Wood's head was ringing and his throat was raw when he checked the time. 7:40. He staggered away, mumbling, "Hao Zhidao." Then he paused beside a cigar store and threw up in the street.

Gwen was seated in his booth. When Guava saw him stumble through the entrance, she hurried over, led him to the table and helped him settle.

Gwen was surprised. She leaned forward to kiss him. "You've had a few."

He nodded, looked into her eyes and bowed his head.

On the other side of the restaurant, Callie was with a

crowd of her thespian friends. Wood didn't notice her when he entered, but she noticed him.

"Have you ever tried chicken feet?" Gwen peered at the menu.

He looked up, eyeing her miserably.

After they ordered, Gwen recapped her time with Raina. Wood managed to control his feelings and hold his tongue. But when the food arrived at Callie's table, her voice rose above the commotion. Wood peered through the diners. Waiters were bringing steaming platters out for the actors. One carried a silver tureen, and he set it down in front of Callie. Wood saw her rise.

"Ruthless," she fumed, staring right at him.

She leaned forward, straightened, and then she was lurching toward him with the tureen in both hands.

"Is something wrong?" Gwen said.

Wood rose to his feet. He shouted and waved, catching Guava's eye.

"Everyone knows—" Callie howled at him.

Wood raised his hands to her.

"—everyone on this stinking island." Callie swung the tureen as she advanced, splashing hot and sour soup on diners to either side. "That smarty bitch—"

Callie reached the booth at the same time as the waitress, planted her feet and swung the tureen, leering in Wood's face. Guava hooked one of her arms, and the tureen tipped to the side, dumping the soup on Gwen.

Gwen screamed. Callie wrenched free of Guava. The waitress slipped in the liquid, reached out, clasped Gwen's shoulder and pulled her down with her.

Callie loomed over Gwen, glaring, her nose switching over the sprawled body like a bloodhound taking a scent. "Another cheap lay?"

"It's the woman I love," Wood said.

"Her?" Callie roared with laughter. She clenched her jaw and slapped Wood's face. "Who wants to have sex with this man?" she shouted. "He's not particular. You, me, Melony on the beach this morning?" She was going to strike him again, but the Hao Zhidao staff converged. A waiter and a busboy grabbed her. Two men in white aprons emerged from the kitchen, racing forward. Together they dragged Callie, cursing and blustering, to the restaurant door.

Gwen wiped the soup from her face and rose. Guava tendered her apologies, picking a cube of tofu from Gwen's hair. Wood stood speechless, staring at Gwen, Callie's words echoing in his ears. Guava faced him, put her hand in the folds of her pink tunic, removed it and slid something into Wood's pant pocket.

Without a word, Gwen turned and stepped toward the door. He hurried after her.

Duval was a phosphorescing nightmare. Bodies flowed past, drowning in the neon river. He caught up to her and clasped her arm. She halted, but she wouldn't look at him; and when he spoke to her, she wouldn't answer. Her brow creased. Her lips parted, her chin dimpled. Then her face collapsed into tears.

"There's something wrong with me," he said. "Really wrong."

She was shaking her head, trying to hide her pain.

"Gwen," he whimpered.

He wanted to put his arm around her. She looked sick, and there were shadows around her beautiful eyes. The look of forever was gone.

"I'm not worthy of you," he said. "I'm not, I'm not."

His chest heaved. She was still shaking her head.

"Don't leave me," he begged her as the sobs rose in his throat.

"How could you," she said.

Her heartbreak withered him. He was only making things worse.

"Grandmother says '*toujours*' is bad luck."

Wood fell to his knees.

"*Adieu.*" Gwen turned and disappeared in the crowd.

There were people in the streets of Old Town, but none like him. They had companions, friends, partners they cared for and who cared for them. Only he was alone. A pariah. An outcast. Then a storm struck. Dark clouds roiled over the Key, and rain came down—lightly at first, and then the sky unloaded. Buffeting winds sent lanes of fog through the streets, empty streets, deserted, abandoned. Wood wandered through them, lost and despairing.

Rain was still coming down. The sky was dark, but a filtered glow, spectral and silvery, lit the drops. He was no longer moving. He stood beneath a stunted tree, with the dead all around him. There were tombs on every side, as far as he could see. The island was a cemetery now—huge, endless.

He was the last of the living.

At his side was a marble angel with a clipped wing. Her head was bowed. Rain drizzled from her nose and chin. Slabs, monuments, gravestones, tilted and cracked; stacked vaults, three, four, five stories high. Iguanas, big as foxes, slid beneath slabs and peered through the tomb cracks like ghosts of the dead. A cock crowed, then another, heralding a dawn that would never come. A man was buried here, Wood recalled, a man who exhumed the corpse of his love and took her home. His desire didn't die with her.

The Seven of Cups. That was his Outcome. A man faced the clouds, lost in illusion. "He'll never find love," Nan said. "All he can see are his hopes and dreams."

He'd been born with a crying need, in a world teeming with people. But he'd cut himself off from them all, become deaf to their speech. From his cloudy hopes, torrents fell, and the life around him dissolved and ran through the streets.

He was no longer Wood the writer, desperate for love. He was a ghost, without a soul or a self.

He thrust his hands into his soaked pockets. One was empty. In the other, he felt a lumpy thing—soft, in a torn cellophane wrapper. When he drew his hand out, he saw a cookie with an unread fortune.

Wood peeled away the cellophane. In the soggy mass, he found a strip of wet paper. Was there anything left to tell?

He stepped out from under the stunted tree and turned, unfolding the strip, reading the fortune in the silvery light. NOTHING IS LOST, it said, UNTIL YOUR MOTHER CAN'T FIND IT.

The silver light came from a full moon. It was low in the sky. The clouds had parted and the rain had stopped. In the gap, against the luminous disk, Wood saw the twin steeples rising from the earth. Our Mother.

All at once, he knew where he was. He could see where the cemetery ended and a fence met the street. He put the fortune back in his pocket and started forward.

The long vines around the cottage were plaited and tangled, waxed by the moon. Wood reached his hands out to steady himself, grasping the stakes of the picket fence. The old house with its rangy tree and overgrown garden shifted before him. And in the center of it all was the familiar face.

Auntie Coco tipped on her rocker, fanning her breast. She was eyeing him tenderly and nodding. She'd been expecting him. She folded her fan and rose, shooing the chickens away. She descended the steps, grasped his arm and helped him through the gate, onto the porch. Then she was opening the weatherworn door, guiding him through.

"There now," she patted his back. "Have you had your crack-up?"

He looked past her inquisitive face. The windows were matted with leaves, the rich upholstery pinned with lace. She was wearing a pilled robe with nothing beneath.

"I loved her," he said.

"Did you?" Auntie was leading him toward the rear.

"Something's the matter with me," Wood said.

She opened her bedroom door. He remembered the brocade chair, the four-poster.

"The Key, its fruit," he shook his head. "Papaya, Gwen—"

The old woman drew him to the foot of the bed.

"Auntie," he sighed, touching the stringy mop of hair.

"Wood," she said softly, unbuttoning his shirt. "You knew to come."

"I'm empty," he said, with a sob in his throat.

Her eyes met his. "You're still my boy."

She removed his clothing, folded back the bedding and eased him down. Then she curled beside him and caressed his head. "Did you think I'd given up on you?" She squinted and smirked, as if she found the idea funny.

"Here you go," she said, moving her robe aside.

A large breast appeared, round and full. The aureole was purple-brown, the nipple stiff. A white drop appeared at its tip. She put her finger to it and touched his lips. The drop was sweeter than cow's milk, and warm.

"I'm tingling," she whispered.

Wood's vision blurred. Auntie was all around him. She smelled like a meadow. He found the nipple with his lips and drew it between them.

Auntie quivered. "It's coming down. Pull, Wood. Pull."

He did as she said, and she gasped and sighed. Inside his mouth, threads of milk emerged from the knobby flesh.

"Go on now."

Wood opened his jaws around the capacious breast.

"That's it. My desperate boy."

Jets tickled the back of his throat.

"Don't let go," Auntie whispered.

Her warmth was on his tongue, filling his throat, heating his chest. He could feel the pulse in her breast.

"We're flowing," she sighed. "Slow, slow— There's no rush. Find your rhythm."

Her breath was moist in his ear. Her arms held him.

Wood relaxed against her. Time passed and a dreamy sound mounted, along with the rocking of tides. A sound that soothed him.

Was Auntie humming? Was it the wind or the sigh of her heart?

I'm on an island, Wood thought. A small one that had lost its mooring. It was free of the Keys now, drifting past the Tortugas, headed out to sea.

The island was Auntie, and he was clinging to her. Her

warm body was the shore of a sandy beach, rippled by wind and sifted by wave.

From his place on the shore, Wood could see: a craft was approaching. A little red dinghy. Without sail, rudder or oars, it made its way forward magically, riding the chop. A pink figure was standing between the thwarts. Naked and pink, with smooth pink skin and a long pink head—an animal head with ears like a donkey. *The Magus*, Wood thought; the creature he'd seen on Nan's card, the Pilgrim's helpmate in the stage show burlesque.

The pink creature's eyes were giant seeds, black and gleaming, and a scutcheon of gleaming seeds patterned its chest. As Wood watched, the creature raised its arms and spread them, three fingers on each. Could it see him? Was it greeting him? From behind its shoulders, triangular wings lifted, bristling with feathers.

The boat nosed into a sand bank. As the creature stepped out, the red dinghy tipped onto its side. The creature was crossing the sand now, its long legs shifting, its long pink tail wriggling behind. It had a smile as warm as the sun. Its eyes reflected the blue of the sky. Its pink feet had three toes each, and as the creature approached, it swayed from side to side, as if gravity was barely holding it down.

Wood felt a welcome in the creature's spread arms and its magical eyes. It saw him. It was headed straight toward him, and it was pleased he was there.

Wood stepped from the shade of the banana palms. The

pink creature's fingers twitched, motioning him closer. What did it want? Why was it here? The creature's jaw opened, and its tongue appeared, as pink as its tail, and pointed and snaky too.

Shall we see? the creature said.

Wood surfaced from a dream or a trance. How long had it been? The air was dark and damp. White candles were lit. The flames cast wavering shadows on walls that looked folded like the inside of a cave. Above him, he saw a head-shaped shadow with three dark depressions—two eyes and a circle of mouth.

Falling stars, sequins of light— Auntie Coco's great breasts hung down, drizzling.

"Open," she murmured. A giant nipple descended, touching his tongue, dragging across it, milk streaming, pooling around his gums.

Her features grew larger, nearer, framed by her stringy hair.

"Latch on," Auntie told him. "Close your eyes."

He did as she said, and the dream resumed.

The sea. The island. The beach.

The pink creature, tall as two men, was nearly upon him. From its armpits, grapes had sprouted. They hung down in thick bunches on either side. Its ears flicked, its nostrils flared. And its wings were quivering. From its pink groin a large phallus rose, the shaft pink and smooth, the swelling glans like an orange fruit.

Shall we see? the creature asked.

Its tail lashed out. Wood felt it coiling around him, gripping him.

The tail lifted him.

Wood rose into the air above the creature's back, then he was settling onto it, feeling the rubbery skin beneath his chest and thighs. The creature's tail cinched tighter, binding him there.

Who are you? Wood wondered. *What's there to see?*

The creature didn't reply, but Wood felt no fear. Auntie's milk had calmed him, and so had the end with Gwen. He had nothing to lose.

The creature's legs flexed. It sprang into the air. Its feathered wings spread and began to beat, and as they rose, Wood felt the wind in his face. The shore and the red dinghy shrank beneath them. Over the beachfront cliffs they soared. Then the waving wings set and they were banking between peaks and gliding through gorges. Wood felt the thrill of speed, and freedom in three dimensions—

Here we go, the pink creature said.

It stretched its pink arms ahead, and its wings folded against its sides. They were diving.

The land below looked brown and lifeless. But as they descended, the air condensed, and the hills and valleys were misted with rain. And as the rain fell, the parched earth drank it up and grew darker.

Closer they came, closer and closer—

The creature leveled off forty feet from the ground. Its smooth body shuddered from head to toe, and as Wood watched, its unearthly phallus grew, extending from between its pink legs, larger and larger, till it reached the scutcheon of seeds on its chest. Its orange glans throbbed, swollen to bursting.

Papaya, Wood thought. The head of the pink creature's organ was *la fruta suprema*.

A fierce tremor. Wood gripped the creature's back. The pink loins shuddered, the phallus stiffened, and the ripe papaya burst open, showering seed onto the damp earth below. The rain of seeds descended, piercing the softened soil like the needle of a tattoo machine.

Who are you? Wood asked again. *What are you doing?*

Sowing, the creature said. *That's my magic.*

They were tacking, doubling back.

Here we go, the Pink Sower said. *Keep your eye on Papaya.*

And again the glans sprayed.

She's a fantasy, Wood thought.

No, the Pink Sower said. *Papaya is real. But she's no one's mate.*

Again they tacked, and again the glans sprayed.

She's the soul of desire, the Pink Sower said. *Your salvation. She's a part of me—the part I share with the world.*

The land below them was changing. Wherever seed fell, the earth was renewed. Green shoots emerged. Then saplings and vines, and trees after that. The dark soil was disappearing beneath a sea of leaves. And then, as Wood watched, on the trembling branches, fruit appeared, dotting the sudsy green with vibrant colors.

My magic, the Sower said, *is the sun and the rain. And all that you see that grows and fruits.* The barren island had orchards now, orchards and gardens, lush and green, with a great bounty of pulp and juice.

The Pink Sower swooped, rolled onto its side, rounded a peak and dove.

It came in low, skimming a hilltop, dipping into a dale. Then it backflapped and landed, pedaling its three-toed feet over the ground.

It unbound its tail and set Wood down.

He clung to the Sower's leg, shaken, straightening, looking around. They stood in a garden carpeted with grass, with fruit trees and vines on every side.

Not a playground for boys, the Sower said.

There were no toys in this garden—no coins, no jacks, no firecrackers to light; no slingshots hanging among the branches; no kites or paper gliders in the air.

Here, the Sower said, *we have real earth, real seeds, real trees. For those who know how to make things grow. Are you a husbandman, Wood?*

The black eyes gleamed, catching the sun. The donkey ears twitched, and the long tail twirled.

It's fertile ground, the Pink Sower said, *as you can see.*

Wood looked down. His feet were bare, and the soil was

dark and soft beneath. As he watched, his toes grew longer. They crept over the soil, reaching out to either side. And then they were sinking, anchoring him securely.

I can't move, he thought.

He raised his arms, waving at the Sower to halt the transformation. But his arms became boughs, his fingers turned into branches. With shock, Wood saw his limbs growing thicker and longer, stubs emerging at every angle. The stubs branched and ramified, again and again. And then, all at once, they leafed out.

A green mesh appeared, arching over his head, hiding the sky.

Here they come, the Pink Sower said.

From the ends of the branches, green fruits started. Small at first, then larger, swelling, big and heart-shaped.

Look at you, the Sower marveled. *A guanabana tree.*

Wood could feel the sap in his trunk, the life in his veins. He was feeding his fruit.

Do you see? the Sower said.

Wood saw. They were more than bright objects in an open-air market. All he had known was the harvest. He could see where they came from now, how they grew, what it took to create them.

There is more to fruit than consuming, the Sower said. *Rooting, providing, caring and tending— That's not a boy's work. It's the work of a man.*

They're yours, Wood guessed. *The fruit women.*

The Pink Sower nodded. *They need soil and sun, seed and rain. And wood too—a nourishing vine or a tree with roots. That's my plan.*

Will you let me go back? Wood asked.

But the Sower had spread its wings, and as the words left Wood's lips, the smooth-skinned god rose into the sky and winged away on the wind.

Wood was still growing.

The increase of years were mere moments—the sun and rain, just a flicker; the ripening, a flashing of colored jewels; the kinetoscope of passing seasons, layers of leaf-fall, the thickening humus, deepening roots and the burgeoning crown. He felt it in his blood and his marrow, all the giving it took, year after year, to bring fruit forth, to create those sweet and magical things that hung from the boughs. Years passed, and the wood grew older, furrowed, ancient. And at last, some time before dawn, he entered the sleep of the trees.

Candles stood on Auntie's lowboy. The memory of the flames still burned in Wood's mind, but the candles themselves had snuffed out in the night. He felt Auntie's breasts on his chest. She was kissing his head, honoring the images inside it.

"Did you have your little moment with Papaya?" she said.

He drew back and gazed at her.

"I knew you'd find your way to me," Auntie said.

A different woman, completely different. Her brow and nose were as thick, her hair as stringy, and eyeliner was tarred across her cheek. But her face was rosy, her eyes were deep. And the lips—always so immune to disregard, wet with booze and an oblivious smile—now had no smile at all. Their gravity and calm was the mark of patience and a heart that knew it would somehow prevail.

They were in her attic, in a fort of pillows by the window. Mixed with his memories of life as a tree was the memory of Auntie's last feeding. It had been first light, the time of secrets; they nursed as the sun rose from the sea. Auntie's milk was malty by then, like melted ice cream.

"Are you alright?" Wood asked. Her hand was knobby, frail with age.

Auntie nodded. "Drained, but happy. Thanks for asking."

He thought of Gwen. And Piña and Tamarind, Nan and Pumelo—all the women he'd met. They had all been so generous with him, but none understood. Not like Auntie. Her breasts were creased and sagging, speckled with age. He bent and kissed them.

"I'm going to stay on the Key," Wood said. "I want to take care of you."

She stroked his head. "What an idea."

"My night with Auntie." Wood smiled.

"Was one enough?" she asked. "Are you full?"

He nodded.

When they descended, Wood found her robe and put it on her. He raised the frayed collar, remembering the queen of Fantasy Fest on the throne of her float. Then he dressed and they had something to eat together.

"I was married once," Wood said.

"I guessed that."

"She had so little to give. And what she gave cost her dearly."

Auntie pursed her lips.

"She was as empty as I was," he said.

Auntie kissed him goodbye on the porch—a peck on his cheek that seemed to signal a new restraint.

"What are you thinking?" she asked.

"I have to get Gwen back."

"Go to the women," she said.

Wood thought about what he'd done. "They won't help me."

"Wood, go to the women."

He followed Auntie's advice and went to the women, and to his surprise they offered to help. But each of them gave him different advice. Mango thought presents might work. Bijou thought he should give Gwen time. Mamey and Nan told him he had to explain why he'd strayed, but they had different ideas about how he should do that. Then Wood got his own idea, and when he talked it over with Piña, she agreed. He convinced Bijou and Mamey and Nan to assist them.

In the light from her kitchen window, the ring's diamond flashed as Mamey turned the little black box. "It's beautiful, Wood. She'll love it."

"You know her?" Piña asked.

"I've met her once," Mamey replied. "She was sad that morning."

"The rock will brighten her up," Piña said.

"She needs me," Wood said. "That hasn't changed."

His phone rang.

"It's Bijou and Nan," Wood said, and he put them on his speaker so they could talk together.

"Gwen trusts Mamey," he said, "and she respects Nan. She'll listen to you. I need you to get her out of her place." He looked at Piña. "The rest will be up to me."

They gathered in the street outside Gwen's apartment. One end was blocked by Piña's beater, the other by Tray's sports car. Wood stood facing her porch, wearing a pink nylon robe on loan from Mamey. With the sheeny cloth belted around him, he looked like a fighter about to enter the ring. Bijou and Nan were on his left, Mamey and Piña on his right. Tray was on the far side of the street, checking his watch. He signaled, waving his arm.

Wood glanced at the women. Then he raised the whistle that hung from his neck and blew it. "Come out here," he shouted at the bedroom window.

The curtain, half-cocked, fell back into place.

"I'm not leaving," Wood yelled.

The six of them watched and waited.

"Ever," he shouted.

Silence.

"I wish I had more to give." Wood spoke to the curtained window. "As a boy, I was needy. As a man— My struggle's not over. But I understand. I know what I want. I know where I'm going. What I had, what I have now, and whatever the future may bring— Everything, Gwen, belongs to you."

They watched for movement at a door or window. The quiet stretched out.

Wood nodded to Mamey.

"He's sincere," Mamey shouted. "I know him, Gwen."

"You can trust the cards," Nan joined in. "They don't lie. Wood's the man who rides the white horse. I'm sure of it."

More waiting, more quiet. Wood motioned to Bijou.

She approached the front door, rang the bell and knocked.

"Gwen," Wood shouted, "please."

"Gwen," Piña took up the cry. "Gwen," Nan and Bijou

chorused, and Tray added his voice from across the street. And then, strangely, other voices sounded. "Gwen, Gwen. Come on, Gwen. Open the window."

Wood turned. Familiar faces were moving toward him.

Guava strode down the street, grave as ever, fixed on Gwen's upper story. "Give Wood a chance." Sapodilla pulled up on a bike. "Gwen," she cried. And behind her, Mango came jogging in a skimpy bikini. "Gwen, Gwen—what are you waiting for?" Annona rounded the corner, and Fig and Cashew followed. "Shake it loose, Gwen," Piña shouted, and the throng of voices mounted.

Someone grabbed Wood's shoulder. When he turned, Pumelo greeted him with an energetic hug. "How *are* you? How *are* you?"

"We're about to find out," he said.

"Are all these people your friends?"

"I guess they are."

Tamarind was waving, hurrying forward, flanked by strangers—passersby who had no idea what the hubbub was about. Auntie Coco brought up the rear, winded and hobbling, stopping by Tray to catch her breath. A pink van screeched to a halt beside the therapist's sports car, and the doors flew open. The actors from *The Story of Wood* poured out, in costume. The farmer emerged from the cab, turned to Wood and raised his straw hat.

Then Callie appeared. She was hurrying down the block in a black miniskirt and high heels, trailing a blood-red scarf.

Wood opened his arms, and she threw herself into them, sobbing. "This is so hard for me. Callie, the one who gave you her best performance, who used every trick in her playbook—"

"I'm glad you're here," Wood said, motioning her toward Mamey.

"Gwen, Gwen," the crowd was chanting.

Wood faced the apartment and spread his arms, palms down.

The street grew silent.

A moment of nerving. Three deep breaths. Straight from the heart—

"I'm your Knight of Cups," he shouted.

The crowd watched the apartment, listening, waiting.

"I want to marry you," Wood said.

Pumelo sighed. Auntie clapped.

"If you want him, you'd better claim him," Callie cried. "I'm next in line."

"Is someone in there?" a stranger asked.

Wood closed his eyes. *No sting, no pain*, he thought. *No defeat, no despair.*

"Please," he said. And the throng around him echoed his plea. "Please," they implored her, "Please, Gwen. Please."

But Gwen wasn't coming out.

Wood sighed and looked at Piña. "Go in and get her."

The green-haired woman straightened herself and stepped toward the first-floor window with a brick in her hand. She flung it, and the glass shattered. Piña undid the catch and threw the sash up. Then she hitched herself over the sill and climbed inside. Mamey moved to join her, and so did Nan. "Wait for me," Auntie yelled, hurrying forward.

The chatter rose, and opinions were voiced.

"It doesn't look good."

"They can't force her."

"Give him a chance."

Nan disappeared through the open window. Auntie hugged the sill but couldn't get her knee over it.

"A bold move," Mango said.

"He has a beautiful ring for her," Cashew explained.

"Does she know who he is?" a stranger asked.

Guava raised her voice, encouraging Wood. "LET LOVE BE YOUR GUIDING STAR," she said, quoting the wisdom of the cookies. "THE FUTURE SMILES ON AN EARNEST HEART."

Tamarind pointed. A hush came over the crowd.

The knob on the front door was turning.

The door swung open and Gwen appeared, hiding her face with her hand. Piña was on one side, holding her arm, and Nan was on the other. Mamey and Auntie followed behind.

Wood was smiling. The cortege stopped in the middle of the street, eight feet away. He had a speech prepared, but when he opened his mouth, the words escaped him. He reached into the robe's pocket and brought out the little black box.

"Put your hand down," Callie shouted to Gwen.

Wood stepped forward. Could she see? He opened the little box and showed her the rings.

"THIS IS YOUR DAY," Guava said. "DON'T BE AFRAID." And "IT'S TIME. PUT YOURSELF ON THE LINE."

"She's going to take it," Mamey muttered to Nan.

But Gwen's hand remained over her eyes.

"Not looking good," a stranger observed.

Wood returned the ring box to his pocket.

Pumelo cried, "He was wronged."

Annona stepped forward. "He was drowning in failure."

"He was hungry," Auntie explained. "Starving, empty."

"A good actor," Callie said, "who didn't know his part."

A disturbance erupted at the end of the block—a car screeched to a halt beside Piña's beater, and a burly man piled out. He pushed through the crowd, shouting and waving a black revolver. The crowd parted before him. Shrieks and cries. He fired a shot over their heads. Gwen peered through her fingers. Wood froze.

"Son of a bitch," Piña hissed as the ape-man approached.

He halted a few feet from her, lips quivering, shoulders shaking.

"You're not wanted here," she snarled.

Stubby let out a groan, lonely, heartsick.

Piña clenched her jaw, pointing at the asphalt.

The gun fell from Stubby's hand, and he sank to his knees, sobbing, grabbing her shins.

Wood faced Gwen and untied the pink robe's belt.

He took a step toward her, and the robe fell at his feet.

As one, the onlookers turned and stared. Wood was naked, but there wasn't much skin tone to see. His body was a riot of color. A tattoo of a giant guanabana covered his chest, and leaves and branches wound around his hips and shoulders, crossing his back and running the length of his arms and legs.

"Good lord," Callie gasped.

Gwen's jaw dropped, along with her hand.

Wood raised his arms. "*Toujours*," he said.

That spring there was a wedding in the garden at Higgs Beach. It was attended by a host of local characters, and music was provided by two violinists. The married couple settled in a clapboard house in Old Town, and on the occasional evening when Gwen didn't cook, Guava reserved the booth they liked.

Four years had passed. It was an evening in late October, and Wood and his girls were seated at Hao Zhidao, enjoying the celestial flavors of Mango Chicken, Tamarind Beef and Shrimp with Cashew. Wood's three-year-old daughter rocked in his lap. She wore a pink western bib shirt with silver piping. Dancing boots were embroidered on the shoulder. Gwen paused between chopstick carries to nurse a baby girl.

When the meal had ended, Wood set a copy of his new novel, *Island Fruit Remedy*, on the table. He wrote, *With Gratitude, for Guava*, on the title page. She stood by his elbow watching, and when he handed the book to her, she bowed and put it under her arm. Then she extended her tray. There was a check on it, along with a fortune cookie.

"I want to see Granny Coco," the three-year-old said.

"Maybe next weekend," Gwen replied. "She's working right now."

Wood rolled his eyes.

Guava was waiting. As Wood raised the cookie, his sleeve edged back, and the green tattooed leaves appeared. He removed the cellophane, cracked the cookie open and retrieved the slip of paper. Then he smiled at Guava and passed the fortune to Gwen.

LOVE IS A PRESENT, it said, WITH TOMORROW INSIDE.

Rich Shapero's stories imagine triumphs of the collective imagination. His previous titles, *Balcony of Fog, Rin, Tongue and Dorner, Arms from the Sea, The Hope We Seek, Too Far* and *Wild Animus,* combine book, music, visual art and video, and are also available as multimedia apps and ebooks. *The Village Voice* hailed his story experiences as "A delirious fusion of fiction, music and art," and *Library Journal* dubbed his novels "Powerful and complex." He is the winner of a Digital Book World award for best adult fiction app. He lives with his wife and daughters in the Santa Cruz Mountains.